# OUR Journey IS OUR Own

HEATHER PREIS

Publishing Services provided by Paper Raven Books

Printed in the United States of America

First Printing, 2021

Paperback ISBN= 978-1-7362982-0-6
Hardback ISBN= 978-1-7362982-1-3

*This book is dedicated to:*

*My real-life Bailey—although time and distance have taken their toll, you saved my life when I needed it most, and I will love you always*

*and*

*for Hunter, to honor his life, for it may have been short, but it was full.*

# CHAPTER ONE

*Kat*

Kat stood in the dark foyer and listened. She could hear their argument as if she were standing between them, their words vibrating off the walls. She didn't need light to see; it would have alerted them to her return.

"What did you say to her, Sara?"

"Nothing. I don't know what you're talking about. Who?"

Kat lifted her messenger bag over her head, set it on a long, waist-high side table, and shuffled out of her flip-flops. The thick rug in the entranceway warmed the bottoms of her feet. Her hand slid along the smooth wooden banister as she walked up the carpeted stairs— her footsteps muffled.

"My boss's wife! I saw you tonight at the dinner talking to her. What did you say to her? Did you tell her anything about me, about our personal life?"

"No! Of course not. I didn't know that was your boss's wife. She was just a nice woman who came up and started talking to me about my dress. I would never say anything out of turn about you. That's so inappropriate."

Kat approached their bedroom door, her steps advancing in slower degrees as she closed the gap. She hovered, almost breathless, on the threshold, hand poised to turn the knob.

"Oh, so I'm inappropriate now. I see. You would love the chance to blab to people about me. Tell the truth. You're just waiting for your chance to get out of here, make your escape. You'll tell anyone how miserable you are."

Kat's sweaty fingertips made contact with the cold brass knob. She squinted at the light shining through the crack in the double doors, as if that would reveal their positions inside the room.

"Gregory, stop this. That isn't true. I was just talking to her for a few minutes. She said she liked my dress. She wanted to know where I got it. And then she mentioned how she thought these work functions could get quite boring."

"Boring? You think my work is boring?!"

"No, I didn't say that…she just…Gregory, no, stop, don't hurt me!"

Those were the magic words. Several loud thuds registered in Kat's ears as the knob turned, and the door opened. Kat stood in the doorway, blinking as her sight adjusted to the bright overhead light. Her vision cleared, and she saw her mother's oversized trunk knocked on its side, open, with blankets strewn on the floor. Her mother slumped on the floor nearby, trying to push herself up with shaking arms. Her father stood just outside the master bathroom door, dress shirt unbuttoned, tie loose like a scarf, spittle spewing as he continued.

"You're such a stupid bitch. I told you not to. You know I don't like you going off on your own and talking to people about God knows what. But you did it anyway. You continue to go against me, and I put up with it for so long, but not anymore. It ends tonight. I'll make it so you can't go to the next function. Then you won't run your mouth to anyone else."

Kat's mother looked up from the floor, giving up attempts to stand. There was a red gash in her left knee, and her right cheek and eye socket were already swelling with color. "Kat, call the police."

Kat closed the door. She didn't want to see. But the imprint of that scene had already been stamped on her vision, and while she felt the hallway darkness seep into her skin, her hand started to tremble with indecision. What should she do? Open the door. Find a phone. Do something! The muscles in her legs clenched. Moving and not moving seemed both trivial and impossible actions.

And then, with incredible mental focus, one foot stepped toward her bedroom. Her pace quickened as she ran down the lofted hallway until she reached her door. She turned to look back, almost as if he was coming for her now. She stumbled backwards into her room, slammed the door, and flipped the lock, imagining the dark shadows were her father about to break it down. He wasn't there, and yet goose bumps tingled the back of her neck as if he were standing just behind her. Kat spun a few times, looking for safety in this locked room, and finally backed against the wall. She slid to the floor, rested her head on her knees, and tried to control her breathing. Was he listening?

Kat jerked when a knock sounded on her door and the knob tried to turn. Her mother whispered, "Are you okay?"

"Just go away," Kat mumbled. And then the tears began to fall as a sharp swell of guilt filled her chest. The only reply was silence.

for as long as I can remember, Mommy and Daddy fighting was a normal evening pastime. So was sitting with each of them afterwards when they'd tell me they loved me and that it wasn't my fault. As the years went by, with my brother and I sitting outside their bedroom door to listen in—we thought we'd barge in to save Mom if it got bad enough—I didn't trust their laughter and loving embraces and always braced myself for the familiar angry tones and elevated voices.

Kat stepped off the school bus and stared at the entrance to her high school. She walked across the courtyard to pull open the heavy glass door. In the marble foyer, she looked anxiously at the front office to her right, hoping to see Mrs. Jones, the guidance counselor. She had to call the police today, as soon as possible. With every moment that passed, her mother's bruises would fade more. Her resolve had slipped last night, but she was determined to do the right thing. He had to be stopped.

Kat walked through the halls listening to muffled conversations about plans for the weekend. She saw the familiar dirty blonde hair of her best friend, Hunter, above the sea of students, and her hands started to shake. He would help her, some way, somehow.

Hunter grinned as he saw Kat approach, but when he read her face, he asked, "What's wrong?"

"It happened."

"Come on." He ushered her with his hand hovering over the small of her back, as they retraced her steps to the front office. Mrs. Jones was in the entranceway this time, and Hunter caught the counselor's attention right away. "Mrs. Jones, Kat needs to see you."

The counselor turned at his voice, and her face changed at Kat's anxious expression. Kat was facing Hunter, as his arm draped lightly around her. She stared at the buttons on his red polo shirt. A thread was coming undone on the middle button.

Mrs. Jones said, "I'm quite busy this morning. Can you come back later?"

"I know, I'm sorry, but you really need to see her. Now. It's important."

As Mrs. Jones looked to Kat for confirmation, she noticed the slight tremble of the girl's shoulders and her unfocused stare. "Alright, I can give you five minutes."

"Okay, come on." Hunter nudged Kat in the right direction. The knots in her stomach sent bile rising into her throat as they all crossed the threshold into the counselor's private office.

Kat sat in the chair closest to Mrs. Jones's desk, while Hunter leaned against the wall behind Kat, close but not in her field of vision.

"So, Kat, what's up?" Mrs. Jones tried to give a friendly, unrushed air to the conversation.

"Well, you know about my parents…" Kat folded and unfolded the hem of her shirt. She slowly filed her nail on her jeans.

She glanced up to see Mrs. Jones meeting her gaze. With a hint of feminine sympathy, the counselor replied, "Yes."

"You know how they get sometimes, fighting and whatnot."

"Yes, we've talked about them many times."

"I need to…call…the police." At the last word spoken, Kat looked at the counselor and hoped that she could simply translate all the events of the previous night through her gaze. Mrs. Jones sat back in her chair. Then, after a pause, she leaned forward toward Kat to speak quietly.

"Tell me what happened."

The story spilled from Kat's lips. She forgot Hunter was there and began the tale with the shouts and escalated yelling, and then her hiding in her bedroom, brushing her fingers over the telephone numbers. Should she call the police? Would they arrest him? Her mother wouldn't tell the truth—she never had. But she was the one who told her to do it. He'd be angrier when he was released. She had to do it…right?

The shrill school bell rang, indicating time for first period. Kat blinked as she realized she was actually in the guidance counselor's office, not back in her darkened bedroom. Mrs. Jones gazed at her calmly. Kat could faintly hear Hunter's steady breathing.

"Kat, I have to go," Hunter said. As he stepped from behind her chair, he touched her shoulder. He gave her a slight nod and squeezed her knee on his way out. Kat didn't flinch. She felt numb.

Kat had managed to tell her whole story without a single tear falling. But as the bolt of the office door clicked shut behind Hunter, her eyes clouded with moisture. Kat bent at the waist, covered her face with her hands to stifle her sobs, and whispered, "What am I going to do?"

Mrs. Jones nudged her tissue box closer to Kat and said, "I don't think you should call the police. You did the right thing last night."

"What?" Kat looked up, her tears shining in the fluorescent lighting.

"Honestly, I know you are hurting right now, but I only think it will make the situation worse by involving the police. He'll only get angrier if they arrest him."

"I understand." Kat wiped her damp cheeks with a tissue and blew her nose, balling the used tissue in her hand.

"What about your brother? Have you reached out to Bailey?"

"He's at college. What can he do? He'd just freak out, come home, and get in a fight with them."

"Does he make it worse?"

"No, he tries to protect me. He tries to change them—to make them see how they are. But they'll never understand."

"Maybe it would help you to talk to him. He can tell you how life gets better when you have distance from your parents."

"Maybe."

"Are you okay?" Mrs. Jones's expression relaxed, shifting from professional counselor to concerned mother.

Kat shrugged and attempted a crooked smile, her cool façade descending. "I should get to class." She stood and paused halfway to the door. "You know me. I'll be fine."

It wasn't until lunchtime that Kat saw Hunter again. She thought he might avoid her, having heard some of her darkest family moments. With such loving parents, how would he relate? Instead, he walked up to her with one of his soul-searching stares.

"You wanna eat lunch with me?"

"I didn't bring one. I was sort of distracted this morning."

"No kidding. I'll share mine. Mom packed turkey and cheese. I'll even let you have my barbeque chips." He smiled at her. Kat relaxed.

"Sure, sounds cool." They walked out to the juniors' parking lot, and Hunter offered her a hand to climb atop his truck's hood. "Really?"

"Why not? It's nice outside. Would you rather sit *in* the car?"

"No, this is fine. You're just a dork."

"What? Am not. It's manly to chill on the hood of your car. It's like I'm saying, 'this is mine, bitch.'"

Kat giggled and was surprised to feel the natural thrill of just being close to him. She felt safe, as if that girl last night was a stranger or an evil twin. She gave silent thanks for having decided to put on jeans that morning instead of her usual skirt and watched as Hunter walked around the front of his truck to climb up next to her on the driver side. He placed his brown bag lunch between them.

"So. I know you probably don't want to talk about it," Hunter said.

Kat tensed and started to brush her hair in her face. Hunter caught her wrist and pushed her hair behind her ear with his other hand, forcing her to look up at him.

"No, seriously, don't freak out. I just want to say one thing." His green eyes held understanding, acceptance, and maybe a mirrored sense of pain.

"Say it," Kat said.

Hunter let go of her hand, which she immediately placed in her lap and began to play with the strap of her bag.

"I wish you had told me sooner how bad it was, but I understand why you never did. I just wish I could have taken some of that burden from your shoulders. I see now how strong you've had to be, living there, dealing with all of that. So, I'm saying that I'm here, whenever, if ever you need me."

Kat believed he was sincere, and she wanted to admit that she hated being strong. She wanted to explain that, as heavy as this burden felt, it was the only true connection she'd ever experienced with her family. It centered her. Without it, she would fall into an abyss—she would be untethered from life. Instead, she said, "Thanks."

"I mean it, Kat. We've been friends for how long now?"

"Um, since Mrs. Wilson's sixth grade art class. What's that? About five years."

"Exactly. My job as your friend is to be here for you. That is the most important reason for my life." Hunter slid from the truck's hood. He walked back around to her and spread his arms out to either side. "Come here."

Kat slid to the ground, and Hunter placed her bag on the ground at their feet. He pulled her into his embrace by the shoulders. Kat wrapped her arms around his waist and rested her head at his heart. He held her close, tightening his hug. Kat closed her eyes to absorb the warmth, both of his spirit and his body. They stood for several minutes, Hunter lightly stroking her back or whispering to her that he would always be there to protect her.

"You okay?" he asked.

Kat nodded against his shirt. Hunter slowly released her. They climbed back up onto the truck hood to share his turkey and cheese sandwich. After a few moments of silence and several mouthfuls of whole grain bread, Hunter said, "So, you wanna ditch with me?" His childish grin changed his expression and the mood of the afternoon.

> Home is narrow, windy roads and ferryboats, autumn-filled forests and bridges over rivers that touch the horizon, walking barefoot down rickety wooden piers, and sitting tranquilly on Hunter's front porch swing. The wind whispers through the marsh as the evening sun colors the sky...

Kat set her pen in the crease of her journal and combed her unruly dark brown hair out of her hazel eyes. The curls stayed for a mere second and then bounced back, a shadow in her peripheral vision. The vast expanse of the lilac-colored river lapped gently against the pier's thick wooden support beams, one of which Kat leaned against.

The marsh crickets sang their evensong, and she knew he would visit her here soon.

As if conjured by her thoughts, Hunter slowly walked up beside her perch and slipped out of his leather flip-flops. He sat along the edge of the pier, legs dangling over, feet itching to dip into the darkening water.

"Hey there, Kitty Kat," he spoke softly.

Kat's dimpled, crooked grin hid behind the curtain of hair she had let fall upon his approach. She did not look in his direction but replied, "Hi. How was work?"

"Boring. You didn't come by, but I brought you something." Hunter reached into the pocket of his navy hoodie and pulled out a folded napkin concealing a large white chocolate macadamia nut cookie. Her favorite. "Mom's cooking sloppy joes for dinner. Want to come down?"

Kat closed her journal—the pen still wedged between her latest pages—stood up, and unruffled her red maxi skirt. Her toenails were painted the same red, Ruby

Sparkle; Kat slipped her feet into her own white rubber flip-flops. Her ensemble was completed with a white camisole and a not-so-subtle black lacy bra underneath.

Hunter stood, slipped his shoes back on, and held out his elbow to escort Kat back up the pier. She stared at his offering and then hesitantly circled her arm through his. The pier was just wide enough for two, and her fingers dug into his forearm every time the structure rocked from their shifting weight.

Hunter lived just down the street from the pier, and when they entered through the side door of his Victorian home from the pebbled driveway, he bellowed for his family, "Mooooooooooooomm, we're home."

"In the kitchen," came a soft feminine reply. "Hope you're hungry. Go get your dad up in his study."

Kat followed Hunter through the first floor of the house. They passed familiar photographs hung in collages on every large wall and resting on end tables and bookshelves. Smiling faces invited her to ponder each fun family moment. The harsh maroon Oriental rug in the living room contrasted with the oversized chocolate brown leather living room set, where she had spent many comfortable hours over the years. She caught a shadowed glimpse of the old saloon-style piano in one of the small front rooms as Hunter ran up the curvy, creaky wooden staircase toward his dad's study.

Everyone found their seat at the dining room table. Between bites of sloppy joes, Hunter updated his parents on developments in his classes and new schoolyard gossip. Both parents listened with attention, eager to interrupt with questions and give him praise.

His dad was also an animated storyteller, waving his hands about as he shared tales of his new freshman class, but each time, his hand would come to rest on his wife's shoulder, or her thigh, or simply brush her dirty blonde hair away from her ear to whisper a kiss.

Hunter either rolled his eyes at them or kept talking about football practice or the latest drama club prank. Kat sat next to him in silence, absorbing the tingly tenderness of the dinner conversation.

At an infrequent pause in the conversation, Hunter's dad asked, "Kat, have you ever read *Les Miserables*?"

"Yes. I read it last year in an independent reading class."

"Mrs. O'Berry's new class? I heard about that. Good for you. See, kid, you could learn a thing from this one here…reading the classics."

"Whatever, Dad. I cream her in pre-cal."

"Did you study for your midterm?"

"Yeah, a little bit. It's not until Monday, so I have time. Want to study Saturday night, Kat?"

"Sure."

After dinner, Hunter caught her gaze and cocked his head to the side to indicate the front door. Outside, he sat on the porch swing, the hinges creaking under his weight. Kat eyed it suspiciously.

"Sit with me."

"Um…I'm good."

"Seriously, come sit next to me. Just do it." Hunter rested his right arm along the top of the swing. He held her gaze while he waited for her to follow his instruction. Kat slowly stepped closer, trying to weigh whether the swing could support another human being. She sank down next to Hunter, keeping her weight in her legs until she was sure it would hold. Hunter grabbed her by the shoulders, pulling her back against the swing and into the crook of his arm. "So, how is life, really?"

"Decent, I guess. I did pretty well on my science midterm."

"I don't care about school. Tell me about that guy you have a crush on."

Kat looked away from him, brushing her hair into her face to hide the blush. "There's nothing to tell. He's there. I'm here."

"Come on, Kat. Go for it. I told you already: Guys need it spelled out for them. You have so much to offer." Kat made no reply at first. No one had really spoken those words to her before. She started to shift away from Hunter—the close proximity was making her itch—as Hunter pushed off the porch floorboards with his feet to rock the swing. Kat almost tumbled out of the swing; her arms flung outward to grasp for balance.

Hunter chuckled and grabbed her by the waist to pull her back and more securely onto the wooden bench. "You're such a klutz," Hunter said as he leaned into her for a moment but then straightened back before Kat squirmed away.

"I am not a klutz. Well, okay, yes I am. But what does that have to do with anything?"

"You attract physical disasters."

Kat was the one to chuckle this time. "Yeah, you're probably right. You seem to handle being around me just fine."

"That's because of my prowess on the football field. I'm light on my feet."

"Bullshit."

"Oh, yeah?" He jumped up, and Kat's hands clenched the armrest and metal chain to counterbalance the shaking swing. Hunter spun around several times and balanced on the toes of his Converse sneakers, embellishing with arm movements like a ballerina. Kat tilted her head back to laugh. With her eyes closed and hands over her heart, she giggled with such carefree abandon that Hunter dropped back to his heels and stared.

As Kat gained her composure, Hunter stood still in front of her. He said, "That guy would be lucky to call you his." His eyes darkened, and Kat's cheeks started to turn pink once again.

Hunter touched her arm and said, "Come on, I'll drive you home."

The short fifteen-minute drive took them just over the county line. Hunter kept up his banter, talking about friends or asking Kat about her classes.

"Photography class was pretty fucking awesome today," she said. "We used coffee cans to expose single sheets of film, and then in the darkroom, we learned how to burn the negative exposure onto photo paper."

"Cool. Can I see?"

"I'll show you during lunch tomorrow. All of my pictures are in the art room." When they drove beneath a street lamp, Kat pulled a camera from her messenger bag to capture the lights and shadows dancing across Hunter's face. He posed for several pictures, making silly expressions at red lights. At the last stop, the signal lit up his smiling face and laugh lines.

I want you to remind me of who I was when you saw me last. I want to remember that I wasn't always focused on getting work done beforehand; that I did have fun a lot. I want you to etch out the lines of my giggles so I may see them again. I want to remember what it felt like to slip under the covers of my bed and the sweet hope of my first kiss. Remind me, if you can, of how you gave me comforting advice when I was lonesome. Of the way the wind blew my hair riding the carnival ride over and over because the drunken carny liked us. Of how comfortable it was to look at you even at the most personal moments. Remind me of the way our fingers knew how to talk. Remind me of how long it took you to break down the wall around my heart. I want to remember the fear in the pit of my stomach when I risked getting in trouble to appease you. I want to remember the contours of your face so that one day when I see you again I will know you and our wonderful past. Keep a list of all the movies we watch and have a tub of cookie dough on hand. You need to know I love you in case I never told you enough or you never knew in the first place. I want to cling to you now like a child clinging to its mother. I think of how you took the place of my brother when he could not always be there. I love your security, warmth, friendship, loyalty, guidance, and most importantly the love you give me in return. If only I could bottle it up and keep it with me forever, for all the years that we will be apart. Maybe one day we'll meet again and we will share our fading memories...

Kat heard her smartphone vibrate on the nightstand at about 10:40 p.m. She moaned as she realized that she had fallen asleep on her history textbook. Her cheek made a ripping noise as it separated from the page, and she fumbled toward the edge of the bed to retrieve her phone.

A text from an unknown number filled the screen, "Hunter Richardson was hit by a drunk driver last night. He died a couple of hours ago. Watch the 11 p.m. news." The breath left her lungs. Kat felt the floor give out beneath her.

What kind of cruel joke was this? Kat tried to think of someone to confirm this unbelievable tale. Another text appeared on her phone. This one was sent from Jake, a guy on the football team; Kat had been his lab partner earlier in the year. This couldn't be true. A heaviness settled over Kat's heart as her vision started to blur.

Kat walked to the den down the hall to turn on the television. She found the Wavy TV 10 station and sat expressionless for fifteen minutes as the night sitcom ended. It wasn't until Hunter's face filled the television screen that Kat's eyes focused and her lips started to quiver. The newscaster spoke of Hunter's young life, his football career, his dreams of going to Virginia Tech, his bereaved parents. As the screen showed pictures of him—in his uniform, at a Christmas party last year, and with blurred-out faces of friends—tears spilled over Kat's lashes. She saw her own t-shirt on one of those faceless peers.

Just before the news segment ended, Kat's mother entered the room to see Hunter's picture splashed across the TV. "What happened?"

Kat looked over at her, tears reflecting in the light of the television. "Hunter died."

"Oh my God."

"I'm going to take a shower," Kat said. She stood and walked past her mother, careful not to brush against her. Kat took one step and then another, making the upstairs hallway seem ten miles long. The walls, white and barren, echoed Kat's impersonal, don't-touch-anything upbringing. She passed several rooms. Throughout the house, the meticulously arranged furniture—with an appropriate splash of color—gave no indication of comfortable hours spent curled up with a good book; the afghan laid along the foot of a well-made bed, its folded corners matching perfectly.

When she reached the bathroom, she closed the door, ignored her reflection in the vanity mirror, and stripped her clothes item by item as though shedding a piece of herself with each one. She turned on the water and waited for it to heat up, standing naked, numb, and almost shivering from the sudden emptiness within her as steam climbed the walls.

Kat stepped beneath the warm spray, and as she ran her fingers through her hair, the full weight of Hunter's death settled on her heart; she could no longer pretend and push her sorrows down deeper. There was nothing deeper than this. The water running down her face concealed a flood of tears, but a strangled cry escaped from her throat. Her knees gave out. Kat crumbled beneath the spray and slid down the tiled wall. Her moans and gasps for air turned to blood-curdling screams as the last of Kat's hope died. Her head dropped to her knees—for once she didn't contain her pain; she didn't care if the whole block heard her because what was the point anymore? How long had she held on praying that someday she would be free of this life, in this house, with the alternating silence and harsh words? Hunter had been her beacon of light in such darkness. Now, she let the despair consume her.

# CHAPTER TWO

## *Bailey*

Bailey sat in the corner of the bar. Over his bottle of beer, he peered at overweight contractors and an assortment of procrastinating college students. The pub off the main street was as full as it would get in the wee Saturday hours. Bailey didn't bother to set his bottle down because he'd only pick it back up—to feel the condensing moisture cool his fingers. Bailey ran his other hand through his wavy, chocolate hair and thought he should get it cut soon; it almost reached his shoulders.

From the kitchen behind the bar, a pair of shapely legs in a pleated skirt sashayed by, the waitress perfectly balancing a large tray with a pitcher of Long Island iced tea. Her green eyes locked on his as her Vans sneakers puffed dust and dirt across the cement floor. Her name was Jasmine; she was a junior art major at College of Charleston, and her dirty blonde hair made Bailey dream of painting and sex, but not in that order. They had met about a year ago when she started dating his best friend, and he'd fantasized about her ever since.

"Hey there," Jasmine said carelessly while setting the pitcher on the table next to his. Her waist-long ponytail slid off her shoulder and grazed his right hand.

"Hello," Bailey said. Before his mind could push away images of her silky, bronzed skin, Jasmine turned away. Damn. As she cocked her hips to miss tables, an older man in a leather jacket reached over from his chair and let his fingertips graze her thigh. Bailey raised his eyebrows. Jasmine glanced sideways over her shoulder but kept walking. The bartender, Christine, glared at the man through eyes coated with dark eyeliner as she poured a drink for an agitated customer.

Jasmine passed by the cop-a-feel guy again to drop off a pitcher of house ale at a nearby table. The man's fingers stretched out again, ready for her leg to swing close enough on the way back. This time, Jasmine stopped just out of his reach.

The man in the leather jacket leaned forward and slid his index finger from her knee up the inside of her thigh until the tips of his fingers disappeared underneath her skirt. Bailey watched Jasmine's face. When realization hit, her mouth gaped open, and then her pretty eyes turned stormy gray. She stepped out of his reach and turned to confront him.

"If you ever do that again, I will take a knife from the back, cut off your dick, and serve it to you on a bun with a side of French fries, okay?" Christine opened the bar door as Jasmine bolted for the back room. Bailey saw her fumble with the latch to the bathroom. The door refused to open, so Jasmine kicked it in instead.

Bailey took a long swig of his beer. Watching the scene before him had been so captivating, he had forgotten about drinking...for a moment. Was it a problem yet? Nah, he'd just turned twenty-one. He'd found the amazing world of sitting alone in a bar with his thoughts enjoying limitless—okay, not limitless—resources of alcohol. Tonight, however, wasn't a night of drunken forgetfulness. It would be a night of intrigue? A night of romance? Ha, yeah right. That ship had sailed. Tonight would be a night of kicking some ass.

Bailey rose from his chair, his legs stiff from sitting all night, and sauntered over to the bar. Christine worked out at his gym. He smiled at her, and she gave the quickest of winks. Bailey leaned back against the bar to better see the man in question. No man touches a woman like that in a public place against her will.

"Hey, you," Bailey said with a practiced air of confidence. "That wasn't cool what you did to my friend."

"What's your problem, kid?" Leather jacket man stood. He and Bailey came to roughly the same height, same build, but from the look of a slight beer gut and his lean into the table, the man was out of shape and on his way to drunk.

"I said I got a problem with you offending my friend here, who is just trying to do her job." Each man took a step toward the other until they were a mere foot apart.

"Oh yeah?" Leather jacket man pushed Bailey's chest, and Bailey stumbled backwards a bit. Five years as a track runner, though, allowed him to quickly regain his balance.

Bailey would ponder later why he still had a half-empty bottle of beer in his right hand. He would wonder at how his muscles reacted before his brain, lifting up and smashing the glass into the side of the guy's face. He would later look at the chicken-feet scars on his knuckles and imagine if any glass had gotten into the bastard's eyes. Unblinking, he watched as shards of green glass crystallized in the air. The guy's face twisted to take the impact, and his arms flailed for support. He found none. He was already off-balance, and the hit from the bottle sent him in a slow-motion plummet to the dirty floor.

Now that the guy's unshaven face wasn't in his line of sight, Bailey could see Jasmine in the corner of the bar, watching the scene play out. Her eyes were heavy with sadness.

Bailey turned and saw a hint of a smile on Christine's face. He saluted to her, dropped the neck of the bottle beside the groaning slump, stepped over him, and walked out without looking back at the beautiful blonde.

Stretching his hand to push the wooden door, he winced at the microscopic pieces of glass stuck under his skin. It was too dark now, near one in the morning, to see the damage. Later, he'd get a rag for his mouth, one for his hand, and a good-sized portion of Southern Comfort whiskey, first to pour over his injured hand and then to chug as the alcohol disinfected the cuts.

"Wait."

The whisper stopped him in the middle of the street. He didn't even bother to look for cars as he turned around. He said, "It's cold out here. You should get back inside."

"I'm fine," Jasmine said despite the miniskirt and light hooded sweater that exposed her midriff, cutting off just below her C-cups. She crossed and inserted her hands into the warm caverns of her armpits.

"Oh my God, you're bleeding," she gasped. Jasmine raced across the space between them, her closeness unnerving him. Even in the chilly night, he smelled her vanilla lotion. Her hands got dry in the winter.

Without looking at his hand, Bailey said, "It'll be okay."

"No, it won't," Jasmine scolded as she took his hand in hers. Then he finally saw. The top of his hand was stained red. Blood dripped from his fingertips and spotted the white street line.

"Seriously, Jaz. Leave it be."

"I…"

"You don't have to."

"I want to."

"No, you don't."

"I heard about your breakup with Zoe," she interjected.

"Please go inside." He took a moment to look up and down the street for cars or a sudden gust of wind to chill her further. Nothing, no excuses.

"Bailey…"

"Jasmine, take care of yourself."

He forced himself to walk away, to forget this girl and his hand until he could get back to his dorm. If he could just find some place that didn't fucking smell like her damn shampoo.

"*You* always take care of me." Her words cut through the short distance straight to his heart. How could he forget?

———◇———

*"Jack, man. We're going to be late to this art thing if you don't move your ass right now."*

"I don't even want to go, Bail. I mean, why do I have to?"

"Because the show starts at 9 p.m. In five minutes. Your girlfriend worked hard to get this gallery spot."

"Relax. We're a few blocks away."

"A few blocks? Dude, King Street at this time of night will take a good twenty minutes. You're leaving your girl hanging."

"Whatever, I think I'm going to dump her."

"Douchebag. Can we talk about why you would want to dump the most amazing girlfriend later? You need to be there to support her tonight. This show means the difference between a degree in art and her future. And I am going to make sure your ass doesn't stop off at Sticky Fingers for some ale."

They could see the King Street Gallery lights from a block away. It was the gallery's once-a-year, sponsor-the-poor-people night, and tonight's lucky pawns were the college art department's finest. Jasmine's paintings reminded Bailey of the Impressionists, what he considered true art. What a shame that America had brainwashed itself into thinking that colored squares could ever represent a fraction of the *imagination it took Monet to do Haystacks at Chailly at Sunrise or van Gogh to create his, yes widely known but brilliant, Starry Night. Jasmine knew colors, understood moods, and felt how each one had a certain stroke. Too bad his dumbass friend would never see past globs of expensive paint on an expensive canvas.*

"Uh oh."

"Let me guess. You forgot the invitation?"

"Yes! Jesus! What is your problem tonight? You're acting as if it's your girl in there tonight showing off her stupid paintings."

"That's because you aren't acting like she's your girl at all."

"Is there a problem here, boys?" said a man dressed in black, clearly offering security where it wasn't necessary.

"No, no problem. Um…"

"Jack! Bailey! I'm over here. I thought you guys weren't going to make it." Jasmine came to the door to rescue them from being sent away. "It's okay, Johnny. These two belong to me." Her smile sealed the deal, but Bailey saw the flicker of disappointment in her eyes. She grabbed Jack by the hand and pulled him into the middle of the chaos. There were *people everywhere; cocktail trays circulated through the room. The bright ceiling lights and shiny hardwood floors gave a backdrop to wall-to-wall coverage of Charleston's best student expression. Bailey felt as if he was spinning. Taking it all in made his head swirl.*

*"Great, isn't it?" Jasmine whispered, leaning into Bailey. She kept a light grasp on Jack's pinkie while he tried to reach for a glass of punch.*

*"Yeah, it really is," Bailey said. Their eyes locked.*

---

Bailey awoke on his dorm room floor, half covered by the comforter he'd grabbed as he'd fallen out of bed. He was still in the clothes from the bar, and he reeked. With his roommate out of the dorm suite for the weekend, Bailey was left to his own devices. His hand no longer had any sensation after he'd burned all of the exposed nerve endings with the whiskey. He pulled his cell phone out of his pocket and dialed a familiar number.

"Hello?"

"Lina. Did I call you last night?"

"No. Why?"

"I smashed some guy's face in with a beer bottle."

"Oh, Bailey, you did what?! Smashed a guy's face in? What did he do?"

"I hit him with my beer bottle, which might I add was not completely empty, because he decided to fondle Jasmine in the middle of her shift last night."

"You went to the bar when she was on shift? What did I tell you? Stay away from her."

"I know, I know. I didn't think she'd be there; she usually doesn't work Fridays. I'm trying to stay away, Lin, but her damn smell is everywhere. Jack is gone."

"It's good that Jack is gone, Bailey. You did the right thing. There are certain limits to even friendship."

"Not ours, though, right?" Why was he talking about Jack?

"Of course. Are you okay? Did seeing her rattle you?"

"You know that I would take a bullet for you, right?"

"Yes, I do. And you know that I would do anything for you. Bailey, you're worrying me. You know that if you say the word I will be down there as fast as my damn shitbox Volvo will take me."

"You don't have to come down. I'm not in a good mood right now. I'm frustrated with life. I think I should just go for a walk or something. I'll call you later."

He hung up the phone, angry at himself for doing so. Nothing seemed to satisfy him. Perhaps a nice walk out in the cold would clear his mind or make him forget for a while.

He took a quick shower, dressed in clothes that passed the sniff test, and pulled on his peacoat and fedora. He had no direction as he stepped onto the cobblestone sidewalk. Where would he go? For what purpose? There was always the library and that imminently looming research paper on Martin Luther for his junior-level Faith Versus Reason seminar class.

Charleston was made for pedestrians. Bailey had known within an hour of visiting the campus that this was the college, the city, for him. After the obligatory introductions and tours, Bailey meandered by himself to the waterline and knew the place felt like home. Not like the home he left behind with the abusive father and helpless mother and younger sister. It felt like a home where he could start to heal into his own person, simply by breathing in the salt-scented air and wandering the one-way streets. He could be responsible for only himself, and he felt a bit of weight lift off his shoulders.

Bailey decided to take the shortcut to the library. As he walked in, he smirked at the young girl asleep at the checkout desk. Her neck would be sore for the rest of the day. He headed straight to the back-corner computer to look up books, on the way stealing a small pencil and piece of paper from the reference desk. The man doing his homework on duty didn't even have time to look up before Bailey was already seated. He wrote down the call numbers for half a dozen books, which began to show a pattern. Heading to the third floor L5000 section was a must.

He stepped into the run-down elevator, but before the doors could close, a small hand blocked them. Intrigue turned to stomach-wrenching regret: Jasmine stepped into the elevator, solemn as usual. She looked first at Bailey's hand. Then she looked into his sky-blue eyes.

"Hi," she muttered.

"How's it going?"

"Decent. Just doing some research. You?"

"Same."

The elevator chimed its arrival, and the doors squeaked open. Realizing that Jasmine refused to step off first, Bailey stepped onto the landing.

"So can we have this out?"

"What?"

Several sleep-deprived people glared at the two over desk barriers. Bailey took Jasmine's hand and pulled her into a study room.

"Okay, what are you talking about?"

"Don't lie. You've been avoiding me ever since Jack left. But don't think I don't notice you follow me home some nights to make sure I make it okay."

"You're right." Bailey sighed and ran his injured hand down his face. "I just can't look at you straight; I still see the bruises," he said. He still remembered how she had looked that night, crumpled on the floor and trying not to cry. "He broke your nose."

"I had to be strong. He hit me to crush me, but he didn't destroy me. I knew even then that you were there for me."

"No shit. I had to be. I know that I did the right thing, but he was my friend." Bailey looked to the floor.

"So you feel guilty for kicking his ass?"

"I don't know. There was a lot going on that night other than me walking in on you guys. The way I was brought up…you should never hit a woman."

"I know, Bailey. I know this, but I've let it go. Why can't you?"

"It still gets me. Jesus, it only happened, what, four months ago. Your nose will never completely heal." "It's healed enough." Jasmine took a step toward Bailey. He tensed up.

"I heard you and Zoe broke up. Why?"

"It had nothing to do with you."

"Tell me why you broke up."

"She got drunk one weekend and slept with some guy from Beta Phi."

"She is a slut."

"Yeah." He smiled for a moment, thinking wasn't that the reason he'd gone after her in the first place?

"You deserve someone better." Jasmine took another step toward Bailey, standing close enough for her chest to graze his torso. She tilted her head up to look at him. His eyes could not leave her face, which seemed to offer something he promised himself he'd never take, he'd never have. Suddenly, he jumped. His coat pocket was vibrating.

"Jesus, Lina," Bailey said into the phone.

"Bad time?"

Bailey looked back at Jasmine, all but leaning against him for support.

"I swear I'll call you back."

"You better." He snapped the phone shut and slid it back into his pocket.

"Sorry about that."

"You still talk to Lina?"

"Of course I still talk to Lina. Anyway, you were saying…"

"I was saying that you deserve better than some girl who sleeps around on you. You need someone to devote herself to you completely."

"No." He took several steps away from her, untangling her arms from his waist. "That's where you are wrong. I will never sign up for the complete control of a woman. I'll never be the sole reason for her existence. Been there, done that, and I'm plenty fucked up because of it."

"Wow, what happened?"

"It's not important. Maybe I'll tell you one day. We're not right for each other, Jasmine."

"Why do you say that?"

"Because it's true. I'm a lot like Jack."

"You are nothing like him!"

"Oh, but I am. Don't you remember?"

He rushed from the study room, leaving Jasmine to stare after him and slump in a nearby chair.

―――――――――◇―――――――――

*Bailey walked the last block to Jack's frat house. They had planned to catch the new Batman movie. He whistled to himself as he took the stoop steps two at a time. He was about to knock on the door when he noticed it was ajar; he could see the hallway phone on the floor with the receiver off the hook.*

*He pushed the door open to find the main room dark and messy. Not frat house messy, but furniture tossed around and drapes ripped messy. A thud came from upstairs. His legs* were moving before he could think. When he reached the top of the stairs, he heard a sound like a baseball making contact with a wooden bat. He rounded the corner into Jack's room.

Jasmine was kneeling on the floor with her face in her hands. Blood dripped through her fingers. As she slowly lifted her head, red gushed from her nose. Her mouth hung open, emphasizing her cracked lips. Her crimson hands fell into her lap, and she stayed motionless, shoulders slumped in defeat.

Remembering whose house he was in, Bailey reluctantly took his eyes off of Jasmine and noticed Jack by the window. His chest was heaving, and his arms were tensed. With hands still balled into fists, his eyes were focused somewhere not in this room. A wire tripped in Bailey's brain.

"What the fuck?" Bailey yelled.

"Oh, God," Jasmine moaned.

"What the fuck did you do, Jack?"

At the mention of his name, Jack turned his head. His eyes were unfocused, "Bailey…"

Bailey lunged across the room and grabbed Jack by the collar of his shirt. "What did you do?!" Before he got an answer, he threw Jack to the floor. Jack scrambled back up and lunged at Bailey, sending both of them toppling onto the bed. Jasmine crawled away from them to huddle in a corner of the room. Bailey bucked his lower body to throw Jack off of him. He punched Jack in the face—a nose for a nose—and Jack stumbled back to slam into the wall. Jack slid sideways for momentary support. His right leg kicked out at Bailey's stomach, but the sole of his shoe barely rippled the shirt.

Bailey yanked the shade off the bedside lamp, ripped the plug from the wall, and turned the base upside down to aim the blunt end at Jack's temple. The blow knocked Jack out cold. His body collapsed to the floor. Bailey raised the lamp to strike the back of Jack's head.

Seeing Bailey poised, arms above his head, Jasmine leaned forward on hands and knees, outstretched one hand to stop him, and screamed, "No!"

When he recognized Jasmine's voice, Bailey's arms gave out, and the lamp fell beside him. His own chest heaved, and blood rushed through every muscle and roared in his ears. He stood over Jack as the rage cleared from his eyes. His hands shook with the sudden surge of adrenaline.

As the memory faded and the stacks of books cleared his vision, Bailey found the shelf with the Martin Luther essays and grabbed the first five in the row. He wanted to get out of there. This damn girl was everywhere. He hit the elevator button a few times as if persistence would make it move faster. When he stepped into the metal box, he let out a sigh of relief. By the time he reached the first floor, barely anyone was left at the tables researching or studying. At the front desk, the book checkout girl had drool running along her cheek.

Bailey dropped his five books on the counter. Startled from her deep sleep, she almost fell out of her boosted swivel chair. Getting out of the library fast had become Bailey's main priority, but the girl wasn't much help. She took her dear old time: rubbed the sleep crap from her eyes, fixed her out-of-control hair, straightened her clothes, cleared her throat, and then realized his books were waiting to be scanned and released.

When she finished, Bailey shoved them under his arm, interrupting her mandatory spiel about a due date, and raced into the cold evening.

He reached his dorm a short walk later and thrust his key into the lock. Despite the effort it took to get the books, he was not motivated to read the essays just now. Before Bailey could finish the internal battle between being a good student and enjoying a free Saturday night, Zoe came out of his bedroom.

"What are you doing here?"

"I came to see you," she said.

He stared at her as if it would make her disappear.

"I want to talk," she added.

"No."

"Come on. I deserve that much."

"You do?"

"*We* deserve that much. We've come so far, Bailey. Gosh, we go back to middle school."

"I knew you in middle school. We didn't start dating until the end of high school."

"Point is we go way back. You don't find a bond like ours every day."

"Were you looking for one with that Beta Phi guy?"

"I was drunk. He didn't mean anything. Besides, you were pissing me off by flirting with that girl downstairs."

"Amanda?! I'm tutoring her in German."

"Well, how was I supposed to know? You could be telling her how to blow you in numerous languages."

"I have never had to tell a girl how to blow me."

"That doesn't mean you don't...never mind. Baby, I want another shot. You can't give up on us. You need me; I know you."

"You don't know me."

"I do." With each word, she moved closer until she placed a hand on his chest. His heart was beating rapidly. "I know that you used to paint. I know that you'd write me love poems." She paused. "And I know that the pain from watching your father...abuse your mom all those years still haunts you. I can still see it in your eyes."

"Stop."

"I know that you walk around trying so hard to let go of those years in high school when you tried to become a man, but he wouldn't let you be one. I know how small that made you feel."

"Stop it." Bailey grabbed Zoe by the shoulders and shook her hard. Her eyes widened; she raised her chin to challenge him. His fingers gripped her flesh, his pupils dilated, and he gritted his teeth. But he saw her fists ball at her sides. His grip loosened, and his eyes slowly cleared as he recognized her face once again. "What do you want,

Zoe? What are you trying to accomplish by bringing up old history?"

"I'm trying to explain that I know the real you, the old you," she whispered, color rising back in her cheeks.

"Exactly, Zoe. That was the old me. I haven't picked up a paintbrush in at least two years; it frustrates me, but I've lost it. And you seriously think I give two fucks about my father anymore? He is a bastard. I have his face and his hands, and he is a bastard. Get out."

"No. Bailey, you need me."

"No, you're wrong. I can't need anybody."

Zoe's gaze softened for a moment, as it had when he'd sneak into her childhood house at night. Often, they'd lie on her bed just staring at each other, unwilling to succumb to sleep and another day.

"Bailey…"

"No, Zoe. The answer is no. I won't hold it against you that you slept with that guy. The shit you put up with by being with me is cause enough for you to sleep around. Just go."

Instead of arguing, she moved to leave. She grabbed her purse and hoodie from the living room couch. Before she passed him, she stopped a few inches away. She gazed up into his baby blue eyes. She kissed him on the cheek and walked out.

Bailey wiped a hand down his face and stumbled over to the couch. He slumped onto it, half hanging over the edge. Blood would soon rush to his brain, but he didn't care. He pulled his cell phone from his pocket and hit redial. "Lina?"

"Hey buddy."

"Help me."

"What's wrong?! What happened? Who was it? Spill!"

"I've had two women throw themselves at me today."

"Oh? Most guys would enjoy that, you know."

"Not when those women are Jasmine and Zoe."

"Uh-huh. I am beginning to see. So was it at the same time? Was your threesome fantasy finally granted?" His lips cracked as they gave way to a crooked smirk.

"Don't joke, Lin. This is serious. I can't go anywhere without them finding me. Jasmine snuck up on me in the elevator at the library, and Zoe was waiting for me in the dorm."

"Ooh, intrigue. I'm sorry, pal. Come see me and get away from your drama for a while, huh?"

"Yeah, I will, I promise. I have fall break next weekend. I get Monday and Tuesday off classes."

"Come! I don't care when, just get in your car and come see me, you slacker."

"It's a deal."

"Maybe we could go into D.C., or are you bored with that after all those dumbass field trips to the art museums?"

"Are you kidding? D.C. is the shit. We can go there and see all the cool stuff. I'll bring up some booze for us, too."

"Yay!"

"What do you want?"

"I don't care, anything. You know I trust you when it comes to stuff like that. You're actually the only person I drink with, if you can call what I do drinking."

"Seriously."

"Hey, now. You put way too much whiskey in my last sour. That's why you got the pouty face and the plea to finish it for me. Those Mike-aritas were good though. Fruity yet subtle bits of alcohol are the way to my heart."

"Disgusting. Speaking of, how is the Boob? I mean Bobby."

"Be nice."

"I am."

"He's fine. He's taking me to a late dinner to celebrate our two-year anniversary."

"Wow, congrats. Where's he taking you?"

"I don't know. Naturally, it's a surprise."

"Well, I hope things go well. You know I support you."

"It's just weird sometimes to think that I might end up marrying this guy. It's not high school anymore. I love him, and as long as he doesn't break my heart before graduation next year, I think he'll be a keeper."

"Just be careful, Lina."

"Always, babe."

"And you know you can't love him more than me."

"I know," she laughed softly over the phone. How he missed that soft sound, hushed in the wee hours when they'd stay up talking, lounging in his parents' darkened living room.

"Oh! He's here! Early! Oh, Bail, I hate to cut this short. You know I'd rather sit here and talk to you than go out with my stupid boyfriend. Oh, flowers! Oh, Bailey, I gotta run. I'll call you later tonight. Go out and have some fun. Bye, love."

Bailey kept his cell phone balanced against his ear long after she hung up. He needed to visit Lina. Ever since that day in the seventh grade when he caught her punching the crap out of the printer in the school's front office, they bonded over art and Quentin Tarantino movies.

Bailey stayed in the same position long enough that he began to relax and wish for sleep. He adjusted his head so he no longer felt his pulse vibrate through his eyeballs. As his eyelids grew heavy and he tried to let go of the baggage from the day, the apartment door opened again.

"Dude, I just saw Zoe leaving the building," his roommate said.

"I know, man."

"Why? You need to leave that carrier of STDs faster than you'd walk away from a fly-infested pile of shit."

"Thanks for that image, Joe."

"No problem. Pizza will be here in twenty."

"Sweet." Bailey's stomach gargled.

"Oh, and I just downloaded the newest version of *World of Warcraft*. You and me; it's on. Let's go."

# CHAPTER THREE

Kat

Hunter's smiling face slowly filled the white photo paper. Kat moved the sheet back and forth with rubber-tipped tongs to ensure the chemicals saturated and illuminated the entire image. Only then could she turn the lights in the darkroom back on.

With the tongs, Kat pulled the photograph from the solution and then hung it with clothespins on a string slung from wall to wall at about eye level. This latest photograph joined others like it, all of Hunter on their last night together. The knot in Kat's stomach had relaxed days ago, but she hadn't regained feeling in her limbs, her heart, or her mind. She drifted through classes without incident; teachers understood, her peers couldn't articulate their feelings, and her parents behaved as they always had.

"Hey, those are great." A classmate, Melanie, flicked on the light in the darkroom. "You really captured him. He must be a fun, happy guy."

"He was."

"Oh, he was your…yeah, I'm sorry."

"It's okay," Kat said, shrugging. What else was she supposed to say?

"So, listen," Melanie said. "Some of the advanced placement art students are having this party at Dillon's house tomorrow night. You should come."

"Really?"

"Yeah, why not? You're cool, and you're talented. You'll belong."

"Should I bring anything?"

"Like what? A keg? No, just yourself."

"Okay." Kat looked away for a moment and then half whispered, "What should I wear?"

Melanie broke into a smile and said, "You're the artist. Anyway, see you there."

Kat tried to smile back.

I miss you so much. It's like you're still here and we are having a fight so I can't see you. Or you're grounded for doing something stupid. I still check my phone like you'll call. Yesterday at school, they emptied your locker, and it was all I could do not to run over and grab the principal to stop him. Those are your things, your books.
I developed those photographs I took of you. To see your smile, your laugh lines, your vibrant green eyes, it was like an icicle being forced through my heart. How do I accept that you're gone? How can I possibly deal with all the shit in my life without you? Should I tell Bailey? He'd just come home.

Kat rang the doorbell to the third house on the left—brick, black shutters, red door—and waited for someone to answer. Melanie opened the door and smiled when she saw Kat. "Hey! Great timing."

Melanie wore her customary hot pink Chucks with skinny jeans, ripped at one thigh and fraying. Her black tank top exposed a small tattoo of the infinity symbol on her arm. She pushed up her red, thick-framed glasses and ran a hand through her short, blonde hair.

"What does your tattoo mean?" Kat asked.

Melanie's smile reached her eyes as she explained, "It's for my boyfriend, Matt. When we first started dating three years ago, he used to trace the symbol on my skin, so I decided to ink it in."

"Cool. Why great timing?"

"What? Oh, yeah. The stash just got here."

"Is that some allusion to someone with a mustache?"

Melanie giggled. "No. The good stuff…the drugs are here."

"Drugs?" Before Kat could change her mind, Melanie pulled her into the house by her jacket.

"Welcome to Dillon's. He's somewhere around here. Beer in the kitchen, booze in the dining room there, and hotties dancing just through that hallway."

"Okay, thanks," Kat said.

Melanie walked off to approach a gangly, tall man with an afro full of curls. She lunged at him, pushing him against the wall to make out. Kat had no idea where to go, what to say, whether to turn around and run. She made her way toward the hotties, as they were the most appealing and appropriate item at the party.

Upon exiting the foyer, Kat's heels clicked across the hardwood floors. She would just have to pretend for a while, and then the party would be okay. Maybe these people wouldn't notice that she was out of place. The music grew louder, the bass thumping along with her heart. Thirty humping teenagers crammed into the family room, moving as a single mass to the beat of the latest Bruno Mars song.

Kat tried to swallow as she scanned the crowd for a familiar face. She caught the unfocused gaze of Kristen, a girl from her history class, but Kristen was a self-proclaimed pot smoker so they'd never mingled socially. Derek and Jonathan were busy in the corner scheming over how to pour more alcohol in girls' drinks. There was one nerdy-looking guy bobbing his head out of tune to the music, and then Kat realized an earbud cord hung from each ear. Weird.

Melanie came around the corner with a wobbly Dillon. "Dillon, this is Kat. Kat, Dillon. Have fun." She departed as quickly as she had the last time. Matt must really be a good kisser.

"Hi, Dillon. Um. Congrats on that award scholarship thing."

"Yeah, totally. Thanks. So…who are you?"

"Er…I'm Kat Johnson. Bailey's younger sister?"

"Ohhh, cool. I think my brother graduated the same year as yours."

"Yes, he did."

"Man, he knew how to party."

"Who? Your brother? Or mine?"

"Whatever. Want some stash?"

"Uh, well, that sounds…I'm good, thanks."

"Your loss. Have you seen…" Dillon glanced through the crowd and then sat on a nearby couch and passed out. Kat sat at the other end of the maroon sofa. Immediately, a redheaded girl without a shirt plopped right next to her, a bit too close for comfort.

"Have you seen my boyfriend?" she asked.

Kat tried to avoid staring directly at her hot pink lacy bra. "No."

"Well, if you do, can you tell him I can't find my shirt? I mean, I remember being upstairs when he took it off, but then I was downstairs with this drink and I walked in here to find him, and I saw you, and you aren't my friend Hilarie, but can you tell him?"

"Sure thing," Kat said, squishing closer to the armrest. The redhead leaned in closer.

"Did you hear about that guy that died?"

Kat froze. Pinpricks spread under her skin.

"It was totally depressing and super sad, you know? Like my mom told me because she's friends with the assistant's assistant in the office, but I was like 'whoa.' I didn't really even know him. I mean I saw him around, and he was totally hot, but like I didn't fucking know him or anything. Just sucks, yeah? Do you know how he died?"

"Drunk driver." Kat said, focusing on the girl's red plastic cup. "Sorry, I have to…" Kat stood up and scrambled away from the girl, dodging bodies until she saw French doors. She needed air. How could they stand this? She was suffocating. The edges of her vision started to blur and fade to black.

> I don't know what to write today. I have
> lost my faith. How can man's goodness be
> rewarded with such grief? What's the point?

"Come here, sweetie. I want to talk."

Kat hadn't spoken to her mother since the night she almost called the police. Since then, Kat had tried her hardest to stay busy with after-school photography or watching football practices like she used to when Hunter played. She has stayed friendly with some of the other guys on the team. Plus, being near the field somehow made her feel like he was close by.

Kat's mother patted the cushion next to her on the steel blue love seat in the formal living room. The sun shone brightly through blue sheer curtains, illuminating the fading green and yellow of her mother's bruises—one the shape of a finger on her bicep and the other a purplish gash on her knee.

"I wanted to see how you were since, well, the other night."

"I'm fine," Kat said. Her face remained relaxed, but her gaze wavered slightly.

"Well, I just want to say that I think it's long past time that we think of moving out." Kat's heart skipped a beat, and she tried to stifle the thrill rushing through her veins. "There's still a lot to figure out, but I wanted to talk to you about whether you'd be okay with that, with us leaving?"

"Yes." Kat almost whispered the word, forcing it out before the moment passed, before the mood shifted.

"Yes?"

"Yes. Mom, I, for a long time, I don't know how to explain—I think it would be best."

"Okay, I'll let you know what I figure out. I'm so sorry your life has been like this for so long. I blame myself. You didn't choose this. I'm just going to need your help staying strong through this. Can you help me, baby?"

"Yeah, Mom. Whatever you need. I'll call people or find a place or get a job."

"No, honey. I'll figure all that out. Just say you love me."

"I love you, Mom," Kat said. She couldn't believe it. She replayed the words in her mind over and over, even as she stared into her mother's calm face. Should she reach out? Maybe hugging her would make her understand that all she wanted was to stand, fling her arms wide, and proclaim that leaving this house would be the best move for both of them. They could reclaim their lives. They could be free.

Dare I hope? I've wanted this since I was six years old, when I first saw the kind of love my parents shared. This co-dependency leads to a self-perpetuating destructiveness that hollows my mother out. They chose each other, but I did not choose this life. Will life be better if she'll finally leave?

I called a hotline once, to ask advice on how to make her see. They didn't have an answer, and their outlook was grim. She has to leave of her own volition. She has to choose me, and herself over him, over his love. I can't fathom it. I can't even begin to understand the kind of love that makes a person need that criticism, need that belittlement. How

sad and damaged does a person need to be
to find comfort in such harsh words and
actions?
I hope we can escape before I become such
a person.

"Glad you could come!" Mel draped an arm around Kat's shoulders, ushering her further in the ballroom of the country club. Despite bailing on the last party, Kat had been invited to another.

"Happy Birthday!" Kat yelled back. Loud music and strobe lights created a staccato vision of the dance floor. Kat saw several familiar faces from the previous party. Matt was mingling and laughing with friends on the other side of the room. He glanced in their direction. What, did he have radar?

"Thanks! Mingle, have fun, maybe even get drunk. You can totally crash at my place if you need." Before Kat could reply, Mel skipped over toward Matt. Stay the night?

Kat wandered over to a long folding table topped with clear bottles of various heights and poured herself a regular Coke. As she wandered back to find a comfortable spot on the wall, away from the dancers' flailing limbs, a tall, muscular guy walked by and glanced her direction. He looked older than the rest of the crowd.

He stopped and said, "Hey. Kat, right?"

"Yes? How do you know my name?"

"My name is Flynn; I'm Mel's older brother. Don't freak out. Mel geared me in this direction because she said you weren't talking to anyone."

"Yeah?" Kat leaned away from him. She wanted to tug on her green tank top or stare at her combat boots. Instead, she fiddled with her rip-cord bracelet.

"That's cool," Flynn said, pointing at the bracelet. "Where did you get it?" The awkward subject change made Kat's shoulders tense.

"A friend of mine gave it to me. Well, actually, he sort of left it at my house. I started wearing it, you know, around."

"Your boyfriend?" Flynn stepped closer. Kat pressed back harder into the wall.

"No. Not really."

"Is he here?"

Kat managed to choke out a curt, "No," before taking a large gulp of soda. Why was this so hard? She wanted to have fun and forget for just a moment about her dead best friend and her stupid parents and midterm grades. She wanted to pretend that she had the control to live this night as if it were her last, because let's be frank, it could be.

Flynn shuffled his feet and turned as if to walk away, so she blurted, "Get me another drink?"

Flynn turned back, eyebrows raised, and said, "Sure." He reached for her red plastic cup. He sniffed at the rim and asked, "Another Coke?"

"Yes, please." Before he walked away, she added, "Put a little Jack in it."

Flynn nodded.

He returned moments later with the cup not quite full. She drank the first half in one long swallow and wiped her mouth with the back of her free hand. "I don't normally drink."

"I don't drink." He said it directly, but Kat didn't detect any judgment in his expression.

"Oh?" She took another big drink from her cup—liquid courage.

"I'm a new recruit for the Virginia Beach police force."

Kat almost spit and dropped her cup. Days ago, she had wanted to call the police, and now they were chatting her up and serving her drinks?

"You okay?" Flynn asked.

"Yeah, just didn't expect that. So how old are you?"

"Old? Hardly. I'm just a year older than Mel."

So she guessed he didn't know about the drugs. Or did he? To be fair, Kat had never seen Mel take any drugs at the last party. She hadn't even really seen the front of Mel's face since Matt had taken her on a make-out road show from room to room.

"Oh, cool."

"Don't worry. I'm off duty. I'm actually still in training. I don't have the authority to arrest anyone yet." He chuckled to himself. After another awkward silence, Flynn gave up, saying, "Well, have fun. See ya."

Kat nodded a farewell and took several more sips of her drink before a trio of art students walked by. "Hey, you're Kat, right?" Geesh, was there a newsletter out with her profile on the cover?

The girls were barefoot in jean shorts and t-shirts. All three cocked their heads at the same angle as they awaited her confirmation.

"Yes."

"We saw your new photographs in the studio. They are epically awesome."

"Thanks. Who are you?"

The girl in the middle with the Team Jacob t-shirt said, "We're Mandy, Cindy, and Wendy." Of course they are. "Come dance with us." Kat opened her mouth to object, but one of them pulled her cup from her hand and placed it on the floor, and then the girl with the French braid grabbed Kat's wrist. They were swaying their hips before the next song started. When they reached the dance floor, they spun Kat into the center of their threesome and then danced in real close. One girl threw both of Kat's arms in the air and held them there; another put her hands on Kat's hips to make them sway to the beat. The third smiled with encouragement.

Even though she didn't know these girls and her nerves were still screaming to run, Kat closed her eyes, let her skin absorb the music so it matched her heartbeat, and danced as if she were just another free spirit. The night passed as if she had danced to the same song with the same girls for hours. Occasionally, a guy would join their little group, but the trio shielded Kat from eager male hands. Another red plastic cup made its way into her hand, and several refills later, Kat noted a foggy haze around the room.

Eventually, Flynn drove her home and helped her stumble up the driveway in the middle of the night—12:56, an hour after curfew. Where was her phone? Oh my God, her mom and dad were most likely calling her, yelling at her, masking their concern with disapproval.

Kat opened her front door, thankful that her parents had never installed an alarm system. Lights instantly filled the foyer and blinded Kat, her eyes tearing up in response. Did Flynn leave?

"Where the hell have you been? And what were you doing? You reek of booze and cigarettes."

"I was…I…there was a party." Kat felt herself sobering up by the second. Her father and mother were standing at the base of the stairs in their robes. Her father's face was quivering, and Kat couldn't help but giggle.

"Hey, Dad, remember that time when…"

"You're grounded," her father said.

Kat's trip down memory lane faded into smoke, and she mentally switched gears. Conversations with her father had become like this too often.

"Fuck that. You want to be like this? Fine! Screw you. This is what you get. I can't take it anymore. I needed a fun night because you two are killing me."

Her mother interjected, "Katherine, what has gotten into you lately? You aren't this irresponsible."

"Exactly, Mom. I'm not irresponsible, so take a chill pill. Besides, I thought we were getting out of here." Her mother's eyes widened. She avoided looking over at her husband. Kat whispered, "Should have known you'd chicken out." Her hands hung at her sides, desperate to fidget or somehow help explain, but the long-suppressed tension boiled up and became exhausting. "Goodnight. I'm going to bed. You can punish me in the morning." Kat shoved her way between her parents and stumbled upstairs to her room. She fell onto her mattress, fully clothed. Hunter's face filled her mind, sending tears down her cheeks before she fell asleep.

I'm suffocating. No matter what I do, it's not good enough. When I try to rebel even a little, I get the harshest reaction. I am drifting through life with no purpose and no direction, only surviving each day through sheer willpower and the faint impression that I shouldn't give up. I don't want to shame Hunter's memory; I lived. I should use the gift of each day to the fullest, but how can I when my parents are so manipulative and controlling? Is it me? Am I just being dramatic? Maybe other teens have to deal with their crazy parents, too.

It just scares me because some days I can sit for hours, not moving, staring at a speck on the wall, and I don't feel a thing. I am so numb to the pain now that I wonder if I can feel anymore, even if some ray of light were to come into my life. I can't even imagine that. Good things don't happen to me. Sure, I've met some new friends, but I'm so wary of them. How do I trust them? How much do I share? I feel so guarded, so much so that I

> don't know how to turn it off. They probably
> think I'm a bitch, stone-faced watching them
> from outside their group. Can they see that
> I'm hurting? Can they see that I am about to
> crumble under all of this weight?

Kat wrote in her journal with a flashlight tucked in the crook of her neck. Words flowed from her pen as if her life depended on it—the release relaxed her. She paused, hand still in formation, to gaze at the stars reflected in the water lapping beneath the pier.

Into one ear, an earbud blasted songs by her favorite bands, but she still felt the vibration from approaching footsteps. Kat's whole body tensed; a scene of her rapid demise flashed before her eyes. She mustered the courage to shine the light down the pier.

She scanned up a pair of New Balance running sneakers, Adidas soccer workout pants, a navy t-shirt with VBPD across the chest, and Flynn's crooked smile. When the light hit his face, he raised a hand to shield his eyes.

"Hey now, I can't see."

"You scared the shit out of me," Kat said.

"Yeah? Do you normally hang out on an old pier in the middle of the night?"

"Nine p.m. is hardly the middle of the night. And yes, I do."

"Fair enough. I was just out for a jog when I saw your flashlight beam in the water. Are you writing?"

"Yeah. So?"

"No, that's cool. What do you write?"

"Nothing. Just my thoughts mostly. It helps. Keeps me from exploding."

"Exploding?"

"Verbally."

"Ah, I get it. I run. A lot. So how come I haven't seen you out here before?"

"I haven't been in a while. Do you live around here?"

"Yeah, sort of. Over in the next neighborhood."

"Nice shirt," Kat said. Flynn's chest puffed out with pride, and he shot her a boyish grin. "You excited to join the force?"

"You know, I really am. I found purpose for my life, helping people. Sure, I'll have to deal with some assholes too, but hopefully I'll get to do some good along the way."

Kat rested the flashlight on the pier, and Flynn stepped closer and sat down cross-legged next to her. "When do you leave?" she asked.

"I got an apartment with a couple buddies from the squad. But I don't have to report for duty for another month," he said. Unsure what to say next, Kat fiddled with her pen. Flynn continued, "You seem different from my sister's other friends."

"What does that mean?" Kat said, shooting a glare his direction.

"Whoa, I didn't mean any offense. I just meant that you're quiet, but there seems to be a lot going on in your head. Like you like watching people from the sidelines rather than getting in the middle. You're kind of a loner, I guess."

"Sure, sure. I get it."

"Seriously, Kat."

Kat's heartbeat stuttered at his soft use of her name. "I understand. I do. You're right. I stay to myself a lot, and I don't really have a lot of friends." Kat swallowed the lump in her throat.

"You can let people in, you know? You can talk to me. If you wanted."

"About what?" Kat asked but looked away.

"I don't know. About whatever brings you here alone at night. Whatever makes you drink at an underage party. Whatever makes you tense up when I get close to you."

She couldn't help but flinch at his words, proving his point. "You don't know me," she said. And she didn't know him.

"You're right, I don't. But I want to. You intrigue me." Flynn slowly reached up to brush her hair out of her face to capture her averted gaze. He tucked the wavy curls behind her ear. Kat's heart began to beat faster, and she wanted so badly to turn and look him in the eye. Flynn traced his thumb down her cheek and cupped her chin to tilt her head toward him. "Who hurt you?"

Kat couldn't stop the tears that filled her eyes as the unspoken answers echoed inside her mind. "I should go home."

Flynn moved his hand to catch a tear as it broke free from her lashes. He brought the damp fingertip to his lips to suck the saltiness away. Kat's stomach clenched with a new awareness.

"Okay, I'll walk you to your car."

"It's about twenty feet away."

"Stop arguing or I'll be forced to take you in for questioning," Flynn said, his lopsided grin catching the low light.

"Oooh, I'm so scared." Kat chuckled as the mood lightened. From the pier, Flynn walked behind her until they reached solid ground. He waved as she got in her car and drove away. Kat couldn't help looking in the rearview mirror as she turned out of the housing area, thinking of Flynn's bright blue gaze.

# CHAPTER FOUR

*Bailey*

Jasmine paced outside of Bailey's apartment door. She looked down the hallway for witnesses, at his door for a sign of life, then back down the hallway. She stepped up to the door and knocked. He should be awake; it was two o'clock on a Sunday afternoon.

In a dream, Bailey heard the knocking as if it were the pounding of his heart. As he stopped running, the sound continued. Bailed woke and threw his comforter to the floor, underestimating the distance from his loft bed as he jumped. Grumbling at being woken, and at twisting his ankle on the way down from the bed, Bailey opened the door. His long hair was unkempt, and his t-shirt and boxers were crumpled. He was the image of "go away." Yet, as his hazy eyes recognized Jasmine, he ran a hand over his tangled mop and straightened his *Simpsons* shirt as best he could.

"It's a bad time?" she asked.

"No, no it's not. Come in."

"No really, I can see you're sleeping."

"Obviously not anymore," he joked. Bailey didn't mind being woken up by a beautiful woman. "Seriously, come in. Everyone in my apartment is gone. Want some breakfast?"

"It's two o'clock in the afternoon," Jasmine said.

"And?"

She followed him into his apartment. Looking around, she noticed crumbs embedded in the dark carpet, empty food wrappers and beer bottles on a small table, and an assortment of wires and game systems surrounding a tiny television. The kitchen, though, was immaculate. "I'll cook."

"Oh?"

"Yeah," he said. "It's therapeutic for me. Gives me something productive to do with my hands." Bailey turned to look at her over his shoulder as he pulled two mugs from the cabinet over the sink.

"That's awesome," Jasmine said.

"So what's your poison: scrambled, with cheese, over easy, or sunny-side up? Wait, you do eat eggs, right?"

"Of course, geesh. What girl doesn't eat eggs?"

"You'd be surprised these days."

"Scrambled, please. And cheese if it's no trouble?"

"I offered, didn't I?"

"Okay."

"Feel free to have a seat at the table—if you can find a spot—while I work my magic. Are you opposed to ham?"

"What?"

"I like to cut some up and put it in with the cheese, too. It adds a nice flavor."

"Sure. I am at your disposal. Feed me."

"Yes, ma'am."

"I'm sorry I woke you."

"It's alright. I should be up anyway. Plus, I was having a nightmare."

"What about?"

"In five years of having them, I'm still not sure," Bailey said. "I just run the whole dream, like I'm running from something. I never find out, I never look back, and I never get a break."

"That sounds horrible."

"Eh, I'm used to it by now. I like to think all that running in my sleep keeps me in shape when I'm conscious."

"You joke a lot," Jasmine said. "Mainly when we're talking about serious topics."

"Coping mechanism. Sorry."

"I don't dream."

"That's kind of weird."

"It is a little," Jasmine agreed. "I have the notion that I dream because everyone does, but I don't remember anything. As long as the rest gets me through the day, I can't complain."

"True enough. Are your days hard?"

"Sometimes."

"The eggs are almost done. Can you do me a favor?"

"Absolutely."

"In the cabinet to my left, there are plates. The toast is also ready. There's butter in the fridge; be careful, it might smell in there."

"I'm on it, boss," she said as she gathered the items. She had to slide beer bottles off to one side before setting the plates on the table. Then she grabbed paper towels.

"Bring me the plates, please?"

"Here."

"Perfect. I hope you like it." He glanced over at Jasmine to see her smirking at him.

"I do," she said.

"You should at least try it first."

"So, what did you have planned for today if I hadn't come over?" Jasmine asked.

"Sleep until my roommate strolled his shagging ass back from his girlfriend's place and then either some good-kid research or some bad-kid drinking."

"I've seen you in the bar a lot lately."

"Turned twenty-one in September."

"Ooh. That makes sense. Happy belated."

"Thanks. How are the eggs?"

"Delicious. You were right; the ham is a nice touch."

"I can cook more than eggs you know."

"I don't doubt it. You'll have to show me sometime."

"What do you want to do today? I say we go out; it's not too cold."

"Let's go to The Market."

"Oh God. Shopping."

"Hey, they have neat stuff."

"Alright, give me five to throw on some clothes."

Bailey retreated into his bedroom for a breather. Why was he going out with Jasmine after what happened yesterday with Zoe? He peeled jeans off the floor and slipped them on. As he opened his dresser door, he caught his reflection in the full-length mirror. His father's face. Then to the side, he saw Jasmine watching him. He closed the door, pulled on a blue-striped button-down shirt and Sketchers, and stepped out of his room.

"You ready?"

"Absolutely."

"Good. Let's go have some fun."

"Let's. And I'm not like those girls who like to shop. After all, I've been at this school for going on three years now. I know where all the good stuff is."

"Sure. We'll see about that." Bailey closed his apartment door, making sure it was locked. At the stairwell, he held the door open for Jasmine to pass through first.

"Thank you."

"No problem."

"So, what research do you have to do?"

"I'm writing a religion paper on the historical context of Martin Luther."

"Sounds interesting."

"It is, actually. I've always been a fan of the big Luther. Plus, his portrait is on a beer label I drink."

"Well then. His awesome rating just went up."

"I'm serious about my beer."

"Trust me, I know. Speaking of, how's your hand?"

"Manageable."

"Okay. How about we skip the basket weaving altogether, quickly scan through the jewelry to satisfy my inner child, and then go right to the interesting trinkets?"

"Interesting trinkets, here we come."

"Where's Jack?" Bailey asked as he and Jasmine walked among the booths at the local market.

"He left."

"What?"

"I went to see him in the hospital yesterday. His bruises were just about healed, and they bolted his jaw together. Ooo, seashell turtles."

"Jasmine, be serious."

"What do you want to know? He didn't say he was sorry, he didn't look me in the eye, and he flat out told me there was nothing here for him anymore. I went back to his room today. He was gone."

"What did the guys say at the frat house?"

"You think I can show my face there anymore?"

"I'll go by later and ask."

"Why, Bailey? He's gone. He hurt me, and he even hurt you. Why are you so loyal to him?"

"It's a guy thing, Jaz. Even if I could explain it, you wouldn't understand."

"Can I borrow four dollars for a Japanese fan?"

"Sure. Are you okay?"

*"Why do you ask? Because I'm completely calm at the fact that the man who beat me is now never going to be back in this town? Because I'm hiding my insecurities by buying material possessions? Or because you are genuinely concerned for my well-being?"*

*"Don't even say that I don't care about you. You know I do." Bailey placed a hand on her shoulder. How many times did he think he should just up and leave this town, start over somewhere new, but he didn't? How many reasons had to do with the woman smiling in front of him?*

*"Yeah, Bail, I do. Don't worry. You are my protector from all evil. What do you think of this bear picture frame for your sister?"*

*"My sister?"*

*"Yeah. It's her birthday this July, isn't it?"*

*"How do you remember that?"*

*"I listen when you talk. No, she'd like this turtle box more."*

*"How do you know that?"*

*"Geesh, Bailey. I was a teenage girl once, too, you know. It was just a guess. Lighten up."*

*"Sure. Sounds good."*

*After she paid the teller, Bailey checked his watch. "I'm going to split and talk to the guys." With barely a grunt of farewell, he turned and walked away, blending into the weekend crowd. He needed to leave. The noise and eager vendors irritated him more than usual.*

*"Bye?" Jasmine watched him turn the corner after ducking under the entrance to the overhead tent.*

---

Bailey hadn't meant to think of the last time he was with Jasmine before the bar fight; he hadn't meant to remember how easily they used to talk. Carrying half her bags of treasures, he glanced at her and saw that same innocent smile. It was amazing what some fake jewelry and sea turtle sculptures could do for a woman's morale and consequently his own.

They strolled toward her dorm building. Their banter had guided them from breakfast through shopping to a small dinner at Sticky Fingers; now they were comfortably quiet. When they reached her building stoop, they paused. Bailey handed over the bags. Jasmine began to twirl them around, looking only at her feet.

"I had a good time today. Thank you," she said to the ground.

"Thank *you*. Believe it or not, I needed you to knock on my door this morning."

"And I guess I was at your door in part for you as well. After our conversation in the library, I felt so horrible at the way you just stormed off, feeling you could possibly be like Jack. You don't have a harmful bone in your body."

"Actually, I did break my forearm playing baseball once. I never regained full use of my tricep."

"Always with the joking."

"Always."

"It's nice to laugh. Sooner or later, we'll have to talk this out."

"On that note, I bid you goodnight."

"Goodnight, Bailey."

At the sight of Jasmine's upturned face, Bailey saw the glow of possibilities. Yet even as his mind traveled a few moments ahead to envision a passionate kiss, he knew it wouldn't happen. Not today. Her eyes darkened with understanding. He nodded and walked away into the evening's fog.

Damn, damn, damn. He had just walked away from Jasmine. That look in her eyes, that "I'm ready" look, pierced his heart. When he used to go out with her and

Jack, he'd see that look in her eyes for his friend. He had watched the way she'd lean into Jack as she got tired or how she'd grab for his hand when she wanted him to stay the night. Damn. His phone vibrated. He wasn't in the mood to do anything but go home and sleep off his regrets.

"Hello?"

" ... "

"Hello?"

"B-Bailey." Now he could hear muffled crying and sniffles.

"Lina? What's wrong? If you don't start talking in five seconds, I'm going to get in my car, come get you, and kill some bitches."

"He wants to take a break. He bought me flowers, took me to dinner, and then told me he wanted a break."

"Bastard. Tell me what happened."

"He said that he knew I'd be the one he would marry, but before he committed, he wanted to take a break to do some soul-searching."

"Lina, soul-searching? I know guys and that means fuck a lot of women before he seals the deal."

"Bailey!"

"I know it's harsh, babe, but it's true."

"I just don't understand. I thought he was different. Two years, Bailey. What does two years mean if at the end of it he still leaves?"

"I don't know. I'm really sorry that you feel this way, but it is ever more proof that you need to move on and get him out of your life forever."

"How do I do that? I'd even planned my promotion around when we'd have kids."

"Oh man. Okay, Lina, just remember tonight and how he's made you feel. Remember it, and don't let him do it again. Call him up right now and tell him to fuck off."

"But he said he still wanted to be with me, just not now."

"Lina, he knows what to say. I'll give him that he knows how to play you. But this isn't good for you."

"Why do you always have to be right?"

"I don't know. I wish that I wasn't, to be honest. But if you knew I was right before, trust me now. I care about you. I don't want to see you get hurt. Personally, your masochistic ways amaze me because you're thinking of going back for more."

"This one is different, Bailey."

"Lina, you just want to believe that so you don't have to be alone."

"Maybe you're right. Because I really don't want to be alone."

"You have me."

"That's different."

"Yes. Yes, it is. But, unlike the trend of men in your life, I will never leave you. I hope you don't question that."

"I don't."

"And I know that you're feeling low because it just happened, but take it a day at a time. Seriously, don't allow him back into your life. You'll only end up back here crying. But know I will be here on the phone or in person for as long as you need me." Bailey steered toward the student parking lot just in case Lina had more to say. He asked, "Are you okay?"

"You know I will be eventually."

"That's not what I asked. Are you okay?"

"I'm curled up in sweats in my bed with the option of a good movie and some hot cocoa."

"Perfect. Go enjoy your warmth and entertainment. Call me later."

"Uh-huh."

"Promise me."

"I promise. Bye, Bailey. Thank you."

"Anytime, baby girl."

As much as Bailey wanted to go to the bar and waste hours at the bottom of a pitcher of Long Island iced tea, a pile of hardbound texts on Martin Luther awaited him. Bailey shoved his hands in his pockets as he trekked back to his dorm. He missed being comfortable, enjoying the color of the sky, being thrilled by the argument in an essay, feeling safe, and not worrying about whether his father's hands could stay in his pockets.

Bailey wasn't surprised to find his apartment still empty of all six guys at nine on a Sunday night. He strolled into his room, checked his computer for new emails or messages, and slipped off his shoes. After grabbing the top book off the stack from the library, he headed toward the lounge. With his feet propped up on the couch, he began reading; but his mind wouldn't focus past the third word. Bailey pulled out his phone.

"Lina?"

"Bailey?"

"Yeah."

"I'm okay."

"I'm glad. Goodnight."

"Night."

# CHAPTER FIVE

*Kat*

Kat was thinking about Flynn. He seemed so pure of heart. He wanted to help people. It was so simple to him. Her smile fell when raised voices resonated down the hall. Her parents were at it again.

"Stop yelling at me!"

"I'm not yelling!" her father shouted. "I'm frustrated with you. How many times do I have to tell you? You never listen to me!"

"I won't listen to you when you're yelling."

"Don't be stupid. You'll know when I'm yelling, but go ahead and keep pushing me, Sara! Keep trying, and you'll see me get mad."

"Oh, big man is here to fight. You feel tough by putting me down?"

"I don't know what you're talking about."

"All I wanted was your help tonight. I always do all the work around here, the cleaning and cooking."

"That's bullshit."

"It isn't. I asked you to do the dishes after Kat and I cooked dinner, and you had to be an ass and say no. After dinner, I wanted to talk to you about Bailey's tuition next semester."

"That boy hasn't proven himself to me, yet. Maybe I'll stop paying his way. Then he'll figure out about life real quick."

"Why would you say something like that? He's our son."

"I'll handle the money for this family."

"Yeah, we're some great family. You're such an asshole!"

"How am I an asshole?"

"Get out!"

"Don't tell me to get out of my own fucking bedroom. You get out. I pay for this house."

"I'm not getting out. You can sleep in the guest room tonight."

"Like hell I am."

"You certainly are not getting into this bed. Get OUT!"

"Okay, now I'm angry. Come here…"

Kat had inched down the hallway until she was outside of their door. She opened the bedroom door quickly. Her father was yanking her mother from the bed toward the door. Her mother half fell and stumbled, but he kept dragging her out. The open door surprised him for a moment, long enough for Kat to say, "Let go of her."

Kat flew at her father. She punched his chest and kicked at his shins so he'd release his grip on her mother. Kat was up against two hundred fifty pounds of solid muscle.

"I…said…let…go!"

It was futile. Kat wasn't even aware if she was having an impact. Her hair swung into her eyes, but she kept flailing out, trying to push him backwards, hoping he'd stumble, that he would retaliate against her.

Maybe this once he'd hit her instead. Maybe then it would be enough to make her see. All he had to do was give her one good slap, and then it would all be over. Even if her mother stayed, Kat could be free. Kat could leave, would leave forever. Just one punch, one bruise. One piece of evidence. One visible scar.

Last year when I was studying for a math test, my father insisted on "helping" me study. I'm not a math whiz or anything, but I usually could follow along well enough. His help was more of a way for him to keep his hand in my schoolwork—a way to maintain control over my school efforts. The yelling usually began when he got more and more out of his own element. I remember he asked, "When did math become more about letters than numbers?" Well, how was I supposed to study when he couldn't proof my answers, but he clearly had the right way of solving the problems?

Or when I wrote my English or history papers, he'd proof them for me, and I never had the right words. It wasn't ever that my words were wrong, at least to my thinking. I had enough confidence to recognize that at least. But his words were always better. The more I fought him, the angrier he became. He'd say my words would lead to a bad grade, and his wouldn't. Then after hours of debating and arguing with him, I would finally succumb. I would surrender the right to my own words. It's the most belittling concession because without our freedom of speech, literally, who are we?

One day I'd had enough, and I gave both drafts to my history teacher the next day at school. What I thought as my first step toward independence was really my first big mistake in the power play. My history teacher called the house to talk to my father about the grading scale and my writing style. I had embarrassed him, and he would never let me forget it. I can't remember the words

> anymore, though his raging voice still rings
> in my head. I thought I could put a stop to it,
> but he came back stronger and harder.

Kat walked into the sunlit foyer. She had spent an hour or so in the darkroom after school, but she had a major history exam the next day and she wanted to study.

"Mom? You home?" No answer. Kat hiked up the stairs to her bedroom, where she threw her backpack on her bed and stared at it with annoyance. History was lame.

From down the hall, she heard a noise like a pill bottle falling onto the bathroom floor. Had it come from her parents' bedroom? Kat padded down the carpeted hallway. Their bedroom door was cracked open, and a dim light seeped through. Using her index finger, Kat pushed it open slowly.

No one was in the main bedroom; the bed was made, the room tidy and neat. The bathroom light was on, but Kat couldn't see anyone in the sliver of mirror visible to her. As she went farther into the room, she heard a soft groan. Kat approached the bathroom doorway. Slumped against the wall, Kat's mother shakily held a pill bottle.

Kat's mom jerked her head up at the sound of someone in the room, a look of fear spreading across her bruised and battered face. Kat gasped. Her mother was unrecognizable; her nose was bent at an odd angle, one eye was swollen shut, and blood coated most of her face and hands.

"Kat..." her mother choked. "Please, help me." Her words were muffled, as if she had cotton balls in her mouth.

Kat stood paralyzed. She couldn't process the image before her. Eventually, the pieces started coming together, and she realized her mother's right arm was braced against her stomach, as if to support it and keep it in position. "What happened?"

"I think I broke a rib. I need to go to the hospital."

"What..."

"Kat! Listen to me," her mother took a few ragged breaths before she continued. "Call for an ambulance. Tell them I fell down the stairs."

"Mom, no. I won't lie for him. He did this? I should have been here. I should have come home right away from school. Maybe I could have stopped it, again. Maybe."

"No, baby. I provoked him."

"Where is he?"

"He went into the office. He has an important meeting in Phoenix tomorrow, and he's really stressed out."

A voice screamed in her head that this was bullshit, this was wrong, this should not be part of her life. How do they get out? Why won't she leave? Does he have to kill her? Will it ever stop?

I'm right back there, right after you died. I feel a gaping hole in my chest where my heart and my guts should be. How can I possibly keep going like this? That man is a monster. I'm done with him. I won't speak to him. I won't even look at him. The second I can leave this house, I will never come back. What kind of man would do this? He thought it made him look stronger—to put down others around him—but it only made him small. Too bad he's a lawyer; no one could ever win a case against him. It's almost like his profession was a choice to cover up the way he is. But he doesn't get it; he doesn't see what he's doing. It will never stop.

Flynn was changing the oil in the Chevy Camaro in his driveway when he saw a pair of jean-clad legs breeze by the car and head toward the front door. As he slid out from beneath the car, he heard what sounded like a double-fisted repetitive knock on the front door. He stood and saw Kat desperately pounding away.

"Kat." She didn't hear him from all the noise she was making. He walked toward her and repeated her name, "Kat!"

Kat spun around to see Flynn standing in dirty jeans and a stained white t-shirt before her. He was wiping his hands on a dirty red rag.

"Flynn…" she said his name as if she would continue.

He raised his eyebrows in response, waiting for more. Kat stepped down the stoop steps and came toward him, hands shaking and tears running down her cheeks; she suspected her eye makeup was leaving marks zigzagged down her face.

"What's up?" Flynn asked, though he sounded a little suspicious, like he was trying to stay casual but alert.

Kat stuttered, "My...Well, you see...I have to tell you..."

"Tell me what?" He knew she was struggling and didn't want to scare her off. He wanted to step toward her again but made himself stay.

"I need your help, Flynn," Kat said. "The other night, you said you wanted to help people, and you're practically a police officer. I don't know where else to go. My best friend died from a drunk driver a couple weeks ago, and I know I shouldn't have been drinking that night you met me, and oh my God do I just ache sometimes for him..."

"You have to tell me about your friend?"

"No," she said. "Well, yes, that's just where I started. There's so much to explain and I'm sort of out of options. I am too damn young to be dealing with this, and my brother is too far away right now, and I just need...an adult."

"Okay. I didn't know you had a brother. What can I help you with?"

"I'm getting there, okay?" Kat wiped her sweaty palms on her jeans and glanced up and down the neighborhood street. Flynn waited. "My friend died, okay, right after I didn't call the police the first time. I don't even know if my brother ever did. I was too young then."

"Call the police? What for?"

"My dad. Come on, Katherine, just spit it out!" Kat reprimanded herself. "My dad hits my mom sometimes, and he did it again, and she's at home right now. I'm supposed to call an ambulance and I just don't know. What am I supposed to do? I know it's the right thing; she needs medical attention. Holy shit, I just left her there on the bathroom floor bleeding. What the hell is wrong with me? And I want him to pay. He's a bastard. And he did this, and I thought maybe if I came to you…I've never told anyone. Well, my friend, his name was Hunter, he knew but only at the…end before he died."

Kat flailed her arms as she confessed to Flynn about her family. She thought she must look frantic. He tried to touch her shoulder, but she flinched and jumped away.

"You have to help me," Kat said. "I don't know what to do. If I have him arrested, I don't know what he'll do. Can they keep him? Can they make him stay away?"

"Well, from what I know, it's her word against his. Will she press charges against him?"

"Fuck. That's the thing, you know?"

"No, Kat, I'm sorry, I don't know."

"Right, well, she won't, at least I don't think she will. She loves him—whatever that means—and she just makes fucking excuses for him. And Bailey, that's my brother, he used to stop it. He was bigger, he could push our dad or stop him or help her. I just can't even look at her face. It's all…" Kat gestured toward her face to indicate the skin and her nose and eyes.

"It's all what, Kat?"

"Broken."

"Okay." Flynn reached out to soothe her again. Kat ignored his touch. He said, "Go home. Call an ambulance. Get her to a hospital. Try to encourage her to press charges. And be careful."

"That's it?" Kat pulled her arm away. She glared at him.

"Kat, I can't really do anything. I'm not involved."

"Yes, you are. I just told you. You're my…you are involved. I need you to arrest him now."

"Kat, calm down," he said. "I can't. And they can't hold him, even if they could take him in."

"What? You aren't going to help me? But I came to you. I don't confide in anyone, and I am literally at my wits end. I am still dealing with their shit. Well, screw you!" Kat started to march away, but then whipped back around to point at Flynn. "Fuck you, whoever you are. I don't need this." She continued back toward the car and began mumbling to herself. "Fine, I'll do it myself. I always fucking do it my Goddamn self. There is no one I can count on."

"No, Kat, don't go. I didn't mean to upset you. I wish I could do more. Let me be there for you."

"Why? Are you going to hold me? I'm numb. I can't feel anything anymore." She beat her balled-up fists against her chest. "But I'm still cleaning up this shit. This is my life; you can't change it. It just is." She was at the end of his driveway. "Bye, Flynn. Thanks for nothing. You're going to make a brilliant cop. Stand up job." Kat half turned and spoke softly, "If my mom dies…I could have stopped it somehow, but he doesn't play fair." Before Kat unlocked her car door, she looked Flynn straight in the eye. "I'm stuck in this fucking downward spiral, and they both have a firm grip on me. The only thing keeping me tethered was Hunter...and he's gone. So why do I even try to stay afloat? Maybe it will just be easier to give in to the freefall."

Kat got into her car quickly and drove off.

I sit here in the dark, cold hospital room, curled up in a chair by the window. The beeps from her body monitors echo loudly in the room, in my head; the flashing lights of cars from the highway below blind me. Like his headlights the night Bailey left. He went to college when I was just fourteen. We were never closer than when we were dealing with our parents. We didn't mingle at school, and his friends picked on me, but I didn't care about any of that. He was there when I needed him to be. He was the shield between our parents and me, and I guess I never realized how much he protected me from until after he left. I am the shield now, but I have so many cracks and weak spots. What happens if I can't hold it together for much longer? We were here, in the hospital, before.

Bailey had told me when he left—I was standing by his car in the driveway, where he was already packed and gassed up for the trip—that I should call him if something bad happened. I didn't have enough forethought at the time to ask him to define "bad." I didn't like calling him; he went from zero to 180 too quickly. And if I'm being honest, when he gets like that, angry at them for acting the way they act, I have a hard time not being afraid of him as well. That's the thing: It's hard to hold onto all that hate and not let it consume you. But as I look over at my mother's swollen face and bruised hands, it's too much. My legs are itching to stand up, walk down the corridors, leave the hospital, get in her car, and never come back. I need my tether, my shield, because there is no one else.

# CHAPTER SIX

*Bailey*

Bailey sat on his dorm room couch, staring at the wall. He held his cell phone a few inches from his face. He could still clearly hear his father's enraged words.

"What are you doing with your life? You can't even stop drinking long enough to go to class. Maybe I should stop paying your bills, and you'll step in line."

"In line? Seriously? What a joke, Dad."

"My father was stern with me, taught me about real life, and I'm proud to say he's the smartest man I know."

"Yeah?"

"You would do good to have some respect for me, boy."

"Sure, I get it. I'll work on that, but right now, you sound like a fucking idiot." Bailey hung up and flung his phone across the room, where it shattered against the wall.

There was a soft knock on his door, and Bailey considered staying still enough to ignore it. When he stood and opened the door, Jasmine leaned against the wall across the hallway studying her folded hands. She lifted her head; he saw confusion and a hint of fear. He couldn't muster a smile to welcome her in.

"Come on in," he said.

Saying nothing, Jasmine stepped by him into the main lounge. She stood in the middle of the room, her messenger bag dangling on her shoulder; she glanced around the room without focus.

"Can I get you something to drink?" Bailey asked.

"No, thanks. I ran into Zoe today."

"Oh, shit."

"Yeah, kind of. She started telling me some things about you."

"Don't believe them."

"I didn't at first. But then I started to remember that night again when you walked in and wailed on Jack. I started to remember how you got into it instantly, and how I had to stop you before you impaled his brain with the lamp base."

"It wasn't like that. I saw you, and I couldn't stand that he did that to you. I don't know why I couldn't stop"

"Bailey, what aren't you telling me? I always thought you were keeping your distance because of our history with Jack. But there's more, isn't there?"

"I don't want to tell you," he said, soft as a whisper.

"What?"

"I said I don't want to tell you. I'm afraid that you'll leave now and never come back into my life. Even as I push you away, I want you here with me. Dammit, Jaz, even back then with Jack, I wanted you."

"No, Bailey, I don't want to hear about that now. Tell me about Zoe."

"Zoe wasn't talking about Zoe for once. She was talking about my father."

"Yes. She did mention him."

"She was talking about my father because for as long as I can remember, he has been abusing my mom."

Jasmine's face showed little surprise.

Bailey continued, "I'm not going to lie to you, Jasmine; I scare myself sometimes."

"What do you mean?"

Bailey sat back on the couch, and Jasmine joined him, keeping a cushion between them. He didn't look at her as he explained, "I've tried hard to separate myself from that life, that version of myself. But, no matter how much time has passed, the littlest trigger will make me that kid again. I pushed you away that day in the library because all I think about when I look at you is your beautiful hair and then what your face looked like that day. I *am* capable of that, Jasmine. I'm my father's son. I know the demon is inside of me, and the *last* thing I want is to repeat his behavior. What kind of a hypocrite would that make me?"

"I don't know what to say…"

"You don't have to say anything. I just needed you to know, I guess. I've dealt with violence my whole life. I don't want to do that to anyone else."

As if the idea just occurred to her, Jasmine said, "What about your sister? Oh God."

Bailey's face tensed. He said, "I think about her and my mom every day, in that house. I left them." He hung his head.

"It was enough for you to protect her."

"No, it's not. I think about them all the time being there with him. I try to talk to my sister. She's a junior this year, and I can't help but think that she will be counting down the days until she can get out, just like I did. The ironic thing is, even though I'm out, I wish I could go back."

"I'm so sorry, Bailey. It doesn't actually do anything to help you, but I am."

"Thank you. I thought I was past it. But now he's like a drug in my system."

"He's still your father."

"That man is no father of mine. I'm so afraid of becoming him, Jasmine."

"Don't let it."

"You are such an optimist. How can you be, after what you've been through?"

"I honestly believe that not everyone is bad at the core. I also believe that you can change your fate if you try hard enough."

"No."

"I'm serious. Let me in, Bailey."

He stared into her eyes, seeking the answers. "I can't."

"I want to help you. I'm not sure how, but it doesn't involve you being scared or pushing me away." Jasmine scooted toward him on the couch. He sat up straight and looked at her with skepticism. "Don't be scared, Bailey."

"Funny. I should be saying that to you."

"Just let it happen."

"Let what happen exactly?"

"This," she said as she leaned in to give him a kiss on his cheek. "I hate to do this, but I have to go. My shift starts in twenty. See you later." She jumped up and walked out the door.

What was he going to do with her? She was certifiably crazy. He pushed himself from the couch and went into his bedroom, mainly because he had no idea what else to do. Sitting in his computer chair, he spun around once for good measure, and checked his email.

Kat had sent a message. He went straight for hers, bypassing spam, junk mail, and important notices from professors. He opened it, and it read:

*Hey bro,*

*High school rocks my socks, and there's this boy I like. Please don't come home and kill him. But on the topic of coming home, you should because mom landed herself in the hospital again. I don't know what to compare it to anymore, but it's bad. Hope school is going well.*

*Miss you,*

*- Kat*

---

*"Go to sleep, Katie."*

*"I can't. I can still hear them."*

*"I know, Kat. Just try to think of something else, and you'll fall asleep. You have school tomorrow."*

*"I can't focus on anything else when all I ever hear is her crying."*

*A knot lodged in Bailey's throat. How could he explain to an eight-year-old that she would never forget that sound?*

*"Try harder."*

*"Don't leave me."*

*"Katie, your bed is too small for the both of us."*

*"No, it's not," she whispered in the dark as she scooted her tiny body over as far right as it would go, teetering over*

the edge. His heart broke a little more; across the dark, he gave her a shy smile.

"Katie, I'm too fat to fit in your bed," he said, puffing out his chest and stomach. She giggled under her teddy bear sheets.

"No, you are not, silly."

"Fine, you caught me." His face grew serious. "But I'm afraid...that if I got in your bed..." She pulled the sheets higher up under her nose, and her eyes got bigger. "That I'd have to tickle you to death." He jumped on her small bed and began tickling her stomach. She writhed in fits of laughter, limbs flailing about and hitting him in the chest and legs. He kept tickling her just to hear that precious giggle.

"Mercy! Mercy!" she cried out between gasps. He stopped and lay next to her after all. She scooted back over a bit to snuggle up against his side, laying her head on his shoulder. They both sighed, and before the noises from down the hall could reinhabit her imagination, Bailey got up, kissed her on the forehead, and left the room, closing the door softly. Before Bailey returned to his own room, he paused outside the door to listen.

"No, no, no, stop. You're going to hurt me!" There was a thud and crash. Bailey skidded to his parents' closed door.

*His hand hovered over the doorknob, as it always did. What could he do? Did it matter? He touched the cold metal with his fingertips, convincing himself that grabbing the knob and turning was the best course of action. He opened the door, and it swung wide. He saw his mother lying on the floor, and her head slowly came up to see him in the doorway.*

*"Bailey...go..."*

*Bailey shut the door again, isolating himself in the darkened space just outside. He went to his bedroom. He shut the door, telling himself it was to keep his father out. He pulled his cordless phone from his desk; he had to call the police. The white phone glowed in his dark room. He couldn't escape his task. If he didn't call, he was a coward. If he did, he would become the enemy. Was he ready?*

***

As Bailey stared at his sister's email, goose bumps spread over his flesh. Had she known that he had just been talking about her, about them? He needed to go home. How? When? Fall break. Lina would be so upset. But she'd also understand. He'd skip Friday's classes to drive home. That way, he would have three full days to stay. He read Kat's message again, checking for urgency. He read right through her calm and sarcastic quips.

"Hello?"

"Hey, Lina."

"Hey, you. How goes it?"

"I'm going home for fall break. I'm really sorry. I wanted to come see you, but I have to go home."

"Well, I could drive home too, and we can meet up."

"You don't have to waste the gas, Lin. I'm going home because I got a message from Kat. It's bad."

"What happened?"

"Same old, I think. But I don't want to take any chances. Mom's in the hospital this time."

"Is there anything I can do?"

"I don't think there is much anyone can do at this point. But I will tell you that I wouldn't mind staying on the phone a bit."

"That I can do. Guess what?"

"What?"

"My parents are going on a cruise for their anniversary. Isn't that hilarious?"

"Actually, yeah," Bailey said. "I wonder if she'll throw him overboard."

"Exactly! And my sister is going with them—with her new boyfriend! How unfair! I have to stay here and study like a good child."

"Sucks like a bitch, don't it."

"Sucks balls."

"We should go on a cruise one day," Bailey said. "Just us kids and not invite the parental units."

"That's a fantastic idea. Where to?"

"Does it matter? Anywhere, seriously."

"It's a deal."

"So, have you talked to the Boob lately?"

Lina hesitated, then said, "No...I'm fine, though. I don't want him to call. It will be easier to make my decision."

"What decision is that?"

"I'm not allowing him to come back to me."

"Good girl. I'm proud of you, really."

"Thank you, Bailey."

"You're welcome."

"So, how's Jaz?"

"She is fine. She kissed me today. She found out about my folks."

Lina gasped. "Oh, God, Bailey. You told her?"

"Of course I told her. Plus, she ran into Zoe earlier today."

"Great. That bitch still at it?"

"Pretty much. Remember I told you she was over here the other day?"

"Yeah?"

"I lost it, in a bad way. It was scary, Lin. I couldn't even tell what I was doing until she looked me right in the eye."

"What did you do?"

"I grabbed her by the shoulders. She kept going on and on about my dad and Kat and my mom and how she knew what I'd been through. She wouldn't shut up, and I grabbed her."

"Oh, wow. Are you okay?"

"Am I okay?"

"Yes. I know that probably rattled you just as much as it did her, the heartless bitch. So I am concerned."

"I'm okay, I guess. I don't want to be like him, Lin."

"You won't. Your soul is too good."

"Are you sure?"

"Bailey…"

"Yeah?"

"I'm sure. For as long as I've known you, it has been your personal goal to protect everyone you could. Oddly enough, all of these people are women. I don't need to guess as to why that is. The point is that you take it personally if you fail at this mission, which is impossible. You can't be there for me all the time or for any other women at your school you've wooed and carried away from fire-blowing dragons."

Bailey laughed, "Naturally."

"So fear not, my friend. You have a conscience, a soul, and a brilliant concept for right and wrong."

"Thank you, Lina. I needed that."

"You're welcome. If you don't mind though, babe, I'm going to run. I promised this girl I'd study with her for our IT exam Thursday."

"Sure thing. Study hard. Stay in school. Don't do drugs. Do not allow the Boob back into your life. And call me tomorrow."

"I will, goofball. You take care, too. And if you don't keep me updated on your damn love life, how am I supposed to know what to call her at the wedding?"

"Wedding? Fuck that, Lina. Bye."

He'd have to make it up to Lina for bailing on the visit. He also wanted to tell Jasmine he wouldn't be around for a few days.

As he left his dorm, Bailey welcomed the brisk evening. They were becoming more and more frequent, odd for this time of year in Charleston. He glanced at his hand, and then remembering, took a closer look. He healed quickly. What had been red, bloody scabs now just seemed to be enflamed veins. He tried Jasmine's phone; no answer.

He turned toward the pub. When he opened the heavy wooden door, loud, infectious laughter spilled from the bar, and Jasmine's natural smile beamed across the room. He'd never seen her so uninhibited or at ease. She turned and saw him, the smile on her face wide and unwavering.

"Hey, I already saw you today," she said.

"I need to talk to you."

"Is something wrong?"

"No, not really," Bailey said. "When do you get off your shift tonight?"

"Bill should let me go around ten."

"Okay. I'll stay until then and walk you home."

"Alright. Do you want some iced tea or SoCo?"

"No, I'll just have a Coke if you can manage it."

"Sure I can. Why aren't you drinking tonight?"

"I don't know."

Jasmine looked closer, but for the first time ever, he did not meet her gaze. Instead, he took a coaster from the middle of a nearby table and waited for her to walk away.

Bailey sipped Coke after Coke while Jasmine finished the last two hours of her shift. She brought them to him without words, most times without even a glance as more people entered the pub. Just before the kitchen closed at ten, she managed to sneak him a basket of fries. He wasn't hungry, but put food in front of a man, and he'll eat. One of life's basic principles.

"Okay, Bailey. I just have to count my tips and clock out. Count to five."

"Word."

Bailey picked up his current glass and downed the half-full Coke. When she walked out from the back room, he paced himself so that he opened the door just as she waved and said bye to Chris and Bill for the night.

"So, what did you want to talk to me about? I just saw you a few hours ago. We didn't say enough then?" She playfully punched his arm. Bailey didn't smile.

"Do you have much homework for tomorrow?" Bailey asked.

"You want to talk about my workload?"

"Yeah."

"Okay," Jasmine said. "I just have a small bit of reading for tomorrow. But for Thursday, I have a poem packet due."

"Sounds like fun. Hard?"

"No, just time consuming. Come on, Bail. What are we really getting at?"

"I have to go home this weekend."

"Oh, that's nice."

"No, it isn't," he said. "I don't know when I'll be back. If it isn't before Wednesday next week, I'll be cutting into classes, and I really don't want to sacrifice my GPA to this whole ordeal."

"Whoa, what ordeal? Why are you going home?"

"My mom's in the hospital."

"Is she sick?"

"No."

Jasmine's expression grew cold. She halted in the middle of a crosswalk. Bailey took a step or two without her and then realized she was no longer beside him. He turned, and she was staring after him.

"Let's go," he called back at her. "It's cold."

"Your father?"

"More or less. It wouldn't surprise me if my sister had actually made the hospital arrangements."

"So what do you think you can do by being home?"

"I don't know, but I have to go. My sister needs me."

# CHAPTER SEVEN

*Kat*

When the doorbell rang early Thursday morning, Kat didn't recognize what it was until it sounded again. Not a dream. No one else was home, so maybe she could ignore it. With her mother in the hospital and her father still out of town, she was enjoying what bittersweet silence the house offered. She was appreciating being home instead of at school; no one was here to make her go, and she definitely needed a mental health day.

Kat groaned. She didn't want to interact with any of the nosy neighbors; her family hadn't come up with a cover story yet. As possible lies formed in her mind, Kat opened her eyes to squint in the early morning sunlight streaming through her windows. Didn't she close those curtains? No, because the dark exaggerated the silence at night and freaked her out when she was alone.

The doorbell hadn't rung again, but now she heard knocking, someone pounding the door with the knocker. What the hell? Kat flung her feet over the edge of her mattress and reluctantly stood up. Oh God, she had to pee. She made a run for the hallway bathroom; she'd deal with the annoying visitor after. Back in her bedroom, she lifted one strip of the horizontal blinds to peek at the stoop outside. She saw a young man, built, in jeans and a brown leather jacket, and blonde hair. Oh no.

Flynn was looking up and down the street for evidence of people. What was he doing here? Their last conversation didn't exactly yield warm and fuzzy come-by-sometime feelings. But Kat couldn't help but touch the glass between them. Flynn suddenly looked up at her window. Yelp! Kat backed away. It was too late.

"Kat! I saw you! Open the door!" The pounding continued. Gosh what a racket. If she didn't want neighbors nosing around, she had to at least tell him to leave.

At the bottom of the stairs, Kat hesitated. She took a deep breath before unbolting the deadbolt. The sun was ten times brighter with the front door open, and she had to block her eyes for a moment to adjust. She heard Flynn before she could see him.

"Okay, so I know it's weird that I'm here," he said. "But it's been a couple of days, and I couldn't take it anymore. Mel texted me that you weren't in school today, and I was worried."

"Take what exactly?" Kat's eyes adjusted.

"I needed to see you," Flynn said.

Kat had thrown her hair into a high bun, tendrils sticking out everywhere. She wore a black Betty Boop t-shirt and oversized blue plaid pajama pants. Her feet were bare, and her black nail polish–colored toes gripped the lip of the doorjamb.

"Um, well, maybe not in such a sexy outfit." He grinned.

Kat touched her hair, glanced down at her shirt, and covered her face. "Oh, yeah." Her lip twitched in a smile, but she had to remember who was on her doorstep. He had to leave. "You should go, Flynn. There's nothing for us to say."

"That's not true, Kat. You had a lot to say last time, and I couldn't process it quickly enough, and could you please move your hand away from your face?"

"No, just leave."

"Invite me in."

"Why?"

"Because I can see an old lady peeking out of her curtains at us having this conversation, and I have something important to say."

"Fine," Kat said, holding the door open with her body. She hugged herself, trying to imagine that she was at least in grubby sweats without any cartoon characters. Flynn stepped into the house but stayed just inside the door. Kat asked, "What do you have to say?"

"No, it's not that easy. I need you fully receptive. How about you go take a shower maybe, get dressed, and we'll go somewhere."

"Why can't you just say it and go?" Kat was growing more uncomfortable. She wanted him to stay, to fill her empty, quiet house with his presence, his voice, his company.

"Because your walls are up in this house," Flynn said. "You'll pretend to listen and then nod me back out the door, and I won't really know if you heard me."

Okay, so he was perceptive, too. Kat brushed a falling strand of hair behind her ear and looked down the foyer to the kitchen.

Kat sighed. "Alright. There's the kitchen. There's a TV in there. I'll be down in a minute." He flashed her a quick grin and headed toward the kitchen.

It was safer if you never opened yourself up to people. It's a lot easier to forgive your own faults, but no amount of happiness is worth the price of that soul-shattering, breathtaking pain of loss or betrayal. It was hard enough to live with my parents every day, never knowing if their nice moods were just another manipulation to be thrown in my face during the next fight. I couldn't trust myself. It was just better not to hope.

Kat came down the stairs again, after showering and dressing appropriately in a purple V-neck and faded jeans.

She was still barefoot, but dammit, it was her house. She turned the corner into the kitchen to see Flynn staring at her white refrigerator.

"Where are your pictures?"

"What?"

"My fridge is covered with pictures of cousins and babies and friends. Invitations? Graduation announcements? Magnets?"

"We don't have any of that." A memory flashed through Kat's mind. Years ago, her father had ripped a large magnet off the door and had thrown it across the kitchen at her mom, who was cooking dinner at the stove. Then Kat remembered the macaroni noodle magnet she had made to frame her class photo from the third grade. She shook her head to clear the images.

"Kat." Flynn looked as if he wanted to go to her, but he had no idea how or what to say. "Come with me. You may be clean, but your eyes are still guarded."

"Taking me out of this house won't change that."

"Please, just give me one day."

"Doing what?" Kat demanded.

"Just one day with me, doing whatever we feel like."

Kat was almost itching with the indecision. Going with Flynn didn't mean she had to trust him.

"Come on." Flynn reached out his hand to lead her out. Kat crossed her arms and walked past him toward the door. She grabbed her purse and shoes and then stood waiting. Flynn shrugged, "Okay, let's go."

While Kat locked the door to her house, Flynn jumped down the concrete steps and ran to unlock his Camaro. He opened the passenger door for Kat just as she approached the car. She eyed him but settled into the passenger seat anyway. He had a great car.

"So, you have your license, right?" he asked after they turned out of her neighborhood and onto the local highway.

"Yes. I just don't have a car. Haven't needed one."

"Whose car did you drive to my house the other day?"

"That was my mom's."

"Having your own car is the best. You can go anywhere whenever you want."

"Or it's just one more thing they can use to control when and where I go." Kat said it before thinking.

"I see."

"Doubt it." Kat studied the changing colors of the trees along the side of the road.

"Hey, don't be like that. You said you'd listen."

"You're not talking."

"Not yet. There's this place I want you to see first."

"Fine."

They rode in silence until Flynn turned the car into the entrance of a park. Kat had been here once a long time ago for a birthday party. He navigated by ball fields, swing sets, and picnic tables before parking at what seemed like the farthest corner of the place.

Flynn glanced in her direction before getting out of the car. He must have expected her to get out, too, because instead of walking around to open her door, he started trekking across a large grassy field. Kat opened her door and followed him.

"Where are you going?"

"You'll see."

"Well, I don't see because that is a line of trees ahead of us, and I am not prepared to go hiking through the brush."

"Quit whining, and come on." Flynn turned toward her and held out his hand once again. Kat ignored it and met his pace. "There is a small entranceway back here that gets hidden by the trees when they're full, but once you get closer, you can see the gravel pathway."

It was true. As they crossed the field, gray stones became visible, and the branches of two trees concealed a path. Kat could walk beneath them without trouble, but Flynn had to duck slightly to get beneath and pass through into the forest. Inside, Kat gaped at fifty-foot trees forming a bright green, illuminated canopy above. The canopy shielded her and Flynn from the sunlight, yet the path was wide enough for four people across. It wasn't dark and scary. It was a beautiful, hidden-away secret. Park benches sat alongside the path, but the two kept walking. They crossed a small wooden bridge that spanned a narrow stream.

Up ahead, Kat could see a break in the tree line. The sun shone brighter there, and she was reluctant to leave this tent of nature. A wooden pier nestled between the pines, overlooking a marsh. A breeze blew through, whispering in the leaves, then through the tall, brown grass and over the water beyond.

Flynn stepped onto the wooden pier. This pier was much different from the one Kat was used to. Land was not far off, but the marsh twisted around and covered the shoreline for miles in either direction, with the occasional house or cottage tucked up on the hills. She heard the popping of bubbles from fish in the water and the chirping of birds high in the trees.

"I love this place," Flynn said. Kat almost shuddered at the shock of his voice. He hadn't spoken since they'd left his car.

"I can see why."

Flynn turned as though to confirm that her icy demeanor was in fact melting away.

"Some of my friends and I used to come here every Saturday to reenact stuff."

"Like in costumes? Those historical reenactment people?"

"Don't judge. We would just come to goof around and beat each other up with swords made of PVC pipe covered in foam and tape."

"You don't anymore?"

"What with all of us going off to college and whatnot, we haven't been out here in months. But I still come out here sometimes for this view. Just to be here—still—as if time could stop."

Kat hopped up to sit along the wooden railing, hooking her feet through the spindles for balance. Flynn approached her, watching her face as he came closer. Damn, she couldn't back up or she'd fall into the water below. He didn't touch her, but he stood just outside the V made with her legs.

"Kat, I wanted to say that I'm sorry about last time we talked. I didn't react the way you wanted, or needed, and I realize now how hard it must have been for you to come to me."

"It's nothing. Don't worry about it." Kat looked away and out at the marsh. She clenched her jaw to keep the emotion at bay.

"It's not nothing. You came to me for a reason, and I wasn't there for you. And if I can convince you of anything today, I want you to know that I won't let that happen again."

"Okay, great. Message received." She nodded.

"Kat, look at me. Please." Kat didn't turn, knowing her fears were clearly written on her face. "You are safe with me."

The simple statement bypassed her thought process, and she turned her head to make sure she heard him right. His eyes were clear, waiting for her reaction.

"You are safe with me," he repeated. "I will never hurt you, and as long as you want me here, I will do what I can to protect you from anyone who harms you."

"Pssh, yeah?" Kat blinked to clear tears that threatened to fall.

"No, don't dismiss me. Stay with me."

"I'm right here."

"You know what I mean. I could feel you relaxing when I brought you here, to this place. I'm here to tell you that, since we first met, I haven't been able to get you out of my mind. I'm leaving in less than a month, and all I want to do is be near you. I want to get close to you, and the harder you push me away, the more I want to show you that it's okay to trust me."

Her shining eyes bore into hiss trying to read his truthfulness. She worried she might start shaking with the tension to hold herself together.

"I...my...you..." Kat's lips started to quiver. She could have cursed herself for showing her vulnerability to him.

Flynn lightly trailed his hand up her left leg then reached around her waist. He stepped between her knees and clutched her in a tight embrace. She wrapped her arms around his broad shoulders, gripping him as if she teetered on the edge of something more than the railing of a pier over the marshy river. The warmth within his jacket rose into her face as she nestled in the crook of his neck. The strength of his arms, and his heart, held her steady.

"God, you feel like home," he whispered in her hair.

Kat lifted her head to peek over his shoulder and replied, "I don't know what that feels like." Tears began sliding down her cheeks. She let them fall. She stifled a whimper when she felt Flynn step backwards, but he brought her with him so she could step down off the railing and gain her balance on the pier. She stayed close, not yet willing to let go of his support. Some kind of gravitational force had ignited between them; Kat had once believed it would be hard to spark with someone that way, but now it felt as natural as breathing.

"Well," Flynn said, taking another step backward. "I'm ready to get out of here. What do you think?" He smiled down at Kat and reached up to brush away a few lingering tears.

"Where should we go?" Her voice was soft. They hadn't said nearly as much as she thought they would. They didn't need to. He didn't understand. And she didn't want to explain it. Not today at least. But for the first time in a while, Kat felt there could be more to life, more to her, than the confines of her family. She felt a stab of guilt, remembering Hunter, but more because she wished she could share this moment with him somehow.

"How about a lazy afternoon at my house. Movie? Blankets? My dimly lit bedroom?"

"Oh yeah? Um, you had me up until blankets. Flynn?"

"We'll take it slow," he said. "I got it."

She thought he would be disappointed, but his dimpled grin gave no indication of a hidden agenda.

"What movie?" she asked.

"I don't know. What do you want to watch?"

"I don't know what you have in your collection. How about *The Notebook*? Or maybe *Pride and Prejudice*?" A smile spread across her face as she wound her arm behind his back, and they walked back along the forest path. "Or how about the latest *Bond* movie?"

"Yes, now you're talking. Tell me you like *Die Hard*, and I'm a goner."

"What about your sister?"

"Mel isn't there. She's with—"

"Matt. Right. You're okay with that?"

"Meh. She's happy. Sure, I worry sometimes that she's too attached, but I think everyone needs a little bit too much love every now and then."

Her mom's bruised form flashed in her mind, then her father's red, enraged face. She tensed beneath his arm.

"I'm sorry." She started to pull away from his touch.

"No, never be sorry." Flynn held his grip firm. "I don't want you to hide that part. I want you to come to me with those stories, if you want. You don't have anything to be ashamed of. I want to know you, Kat." They walked on in silence until they reached his car.

Later, at Flynn's house, Kat discovered that a silent house could still be warm. There was a refrigerator covered in pictures and magnets. Flynn had a problem keeping his room clean; he made her wait in the upstairs hallway for a minute while he threw piles of clothes in the bottom of his closet. She giggled as he threw his body weight against the closet door to close it. He even sprayed Lysol around the room to cover his musty man smells.

Finished with his cleaning attempt, Flynn grabbed Kat's hand and led her into his bedroom. He pointed to the shelves of DVDs stacked in the corner. He removed his leather jacket and threw it over a red beanbag chair. That was the only other seat besides his bed. He kicked off his shoes and flung himself on one side of his bed. With his arms crossed behind his head, he grinned at Kat, waiting for her to choose a DVD.

Kat found the case for *Skyfall* and the DVD player remote, which she threw at him. He managed to catch it before it fell on his stomach. As the movie previews played, Kat moved toward the other side of his bed. Flynn watched her. She sat on the edge, careful not to sink in too deep and tip the mattress her direction. Flynn snaked his hand out to grab her by the elbow and yanked her backwards. She put her arms out to stop her fall, and they landed on his stretched-out torso. Still holding the remote, Flynn circled an arm around her shoulders to encourage her to lie at his side. She complied but stayed ironing-board stiff. Within seconds, the cords in her neck strained from supporting her head.

Flynn lay waiting for her to settle next to him. And with a sigh, she did. Kat shifted her body toward him to rest her head in the crook of his arm, her arms awkward between them. Slowly, her shoulders relaxed, and the movie started. She was falling asleep before the opening credits had finished, and one of her hands reached up to rest over his heart.

I dreamed of the forest and the serenity of the lush green landscape. I walked the trails alone this time, but I felt comfortable, turning down different paths. A bright blue butterfly cut across my path, and I stopped to watch it drift upwards, back and forth through branches, to land on a bush nearby. I wanted to reach out and touch it, even though I knew it would fly away. As I lifted my hand, a twig snapped. I froze.

My heart pounded in my ears; I couldn't hear the birds singing anymore. I thought I heard even breathing behind me, and I pushed my legs to move. I tripped over a fallen branch, and my stomach lurched up into my throat as I fell to the ground, knowing he would get me now.

Wake up.

"Kat, wake up." Flynn shook her lightly. Kat had a death grip on his t-shirt, and he couldn't unclench her fists. He could feel the tension in her body, and she was shaking her head back and forth.

Flynn placed a hand on either side of her face and leaned in to kiss her. What began as an instinctual reaction to wake her up became a teenage boy's stolen opportunity. As tough as she could be in spirit, her lips were soft as silk. Her hands still fisted in his shirt, her legs came to settle around his, and he felt her sigh. He thought for sure she would wake up, and maybe she had, but the transition into a body-to-body make out session was too seamless.

Flynn pulled away just enough to look at her face. The lines had disappeared from her forehead and her eyes weren't squinted tight shut anymore. In fact, her large hazel eyes were looking at him as if he were her rescuer.

"Why did you do that?"

"Uh, you wouldn't wake up. I think you were having a nightmare."

She held his gaze, "Yes, I was."

"Are you okay?"

"Now I am." Kat closed the distance between them once again, brushing her lips against his. He didn't move. He didn't want to scare her away or cause her to stop. But as her lips tentatively moved against his, opening to him and allowing her tongue to run across his bottom lip, he couldn't restrain himself. He ran his hand down her arm and around her waist; he slid a hand beneath her shirt and almost moaned with how smooth her skin was under his rough fingers. Kat reached up to run her fingers through his short blonde hair, and goose bumps rose on his arms as her nails caressed his scalp.

"Kat," he mumbled against her mouth.

"Mmm?" She hooked one leg over his to loop around his waist. He broke the kiss. "What?"

"I should take you home."

"Oh. I see." Kat felt the blush spread across her face and down her neck. She released Flynn and rolled away to the other side of the bed. "Sure, no problem. Sorry."

"Sorry?"

"You've been great today. I really appreciate you being a friend."

"No, Kat, don't misunderstand. I should take you home…before I embarrass myself."

"Why would you embarrass…? Oh." She faced him.

"Yeah. You are still raw, Kat, I know that. I don't want to take advantage of you. And if I'm being honest, I don't want to get too deep into things with me leaving soon."

"Sure, I get it. But here's something you don't know." She scooted inch by slow inch across the bed. "I am stronger than you think. I've been guarding myself a long time."

"I did know that, actually," Flynn said. "I just don't want you to have to guard yourself against me. If we do start something, I want us both to go into it with open eyes, and I want you to let your walls down. I'll wait…"

He leaned in to brush his lips across hers once more. "Besides, you are going to school tomorrow."

Kat groaned and rested her head on his shoulder.

"Come on," he said. "I'll take you home."

# CHAPTER EIGHT

*Bailey*

On Friday, Bailey sat in his Honda Civic waiting for Kat to get out of school. The clock read 2:55. Any moment, the bell would ring and thousands of kids would run out of the doors, ready for the weekend. Hopefully, the brief message he'd left in the front office would get to her in English class before she was released for the day. There was a knock on the passenger window. Who other than young Katie? He hit the automatic button to roll it down.

"What are you doing out of class?"

"Oh, Bailey, come on. We had ten minutes left, and I asked to go to the bathroom. Then I just popped to my locker and slid out by the office. Whatever. Open the door."

He clicked the unlock button. Kat slid into the seat and threw her backpack in the back seat.

"Ugh, I had the day from hell. My history teacher popped a quiz on us after I missed class yesterday, and I didn't sleep well last night."

He didn't need to ask why she hadn't slept. "How's Mom?"

"She's at Obici Hospital."

"How bad?"

"Bad. Let's just go, and you'll see for yourself. I really can't describe it."

Bailey backed out of the parking lot to beat the rush of school buses. Obici Hospital was just five minutes down the road. Bailey parked, and they walked into the main entrance; Kat couldn't quite remember what wing her mother had moved to.

"Hi, we're looking for Sara Johnson."

"Are you family?"

"We're her children."

"She's in East Wing on the fourth floor. If you go down this hallway, there will be elevators on the right.

Take one to the fourth floor and turn left. There should be signs for room numbers; hers is 439."

"Thank you."

Bailey and Kat walked in silence down the hall and riding up in the elevator. The upcoming interaction loomed ahead of them. Bailey felt nervous; the last time he'd come to the hospital to see his mother like this had been so long ago. Usually, his father didn't bother to show his face.

They navigated the halls and found their mother's room. Both hesitated at the same moment outside her door; it was ajar. The low murmur of voices from the television caught their attention, but given how low the sound was, she was either asleep or ignoring it. After they entered the room, Kat stepped forward to push away the hanging curtain a bit more.

"Hey, Mom. Look who came to see you."

"Oh God, Kat. I can't see visitors like this."

"Hey, Mum."

"Bailey! What are you doing here? Don't you have classes?"

"It's fall break. I came to see my favorite mom."

"I'm your only mom. Come here and give me a kiss."

"Yes, ma'am." He slid around the only chair and bypassed her IV stand to lean over wires and kiss her cheek. Up close, he could see the damage. Two fingers on her right hand were bandaged together; one must be broken. Purple splotches covered both of her arms. Her face was the worst: a dark half-moon blackened the top half of one cheek, and her nose had a bandage over it to straighten it—the bone would forever show an evident bump.

"You know what, Mum, I am so thirsty after driving up all morning. Do you need anything: an extra pillow, some ice, anything?"

"No, baby. I'm fine. I got my children, and that's all I ever need."

"Okay, I'll be right back."

Bailey forced himself to walk slowly out of the room and past the nurse's station at the end of the hall. He found an empty visitor's room and slumped against the wall as his hands began to shake. He was hyperventilating. Seeing his mother like that, even though he should have been prepared, upset him more than normal.

He slid down to the floor and rested his head against the wall. How was he going to be able to look at her beat-up face and carry on a meaningless conversation? How could Kat do it? She lived with them; he'd forgotten how numb and detached he'd become when it surrounded him. He would have to bite his tongue and deal with it. However, it would be harder for him now to go home and look his father in the eye. What kind of man could do that to his wife?

Bailey wiped away tears that threatened to fall and took several deep breaths. Leaving the room, he almost turned the wrong way down the hall until he remembered that her room number was 439. When he returned, Kat's infectious giggles were making his mother smile as best she could, crookedly. He could see a few missing teeth in the back of her mouth, where his father had caught the corner of her jaw.

"Mom, you'll never believe it. The soda machine on this floor is out of order."

"Do you want me to call the nurse?"

"Oh no. They are here to help you, not me. I'll be okay."

"Alright. Kat was just telling me about her day."

"Yeah, she told me in the car. I want to talk about you, Mom. What happened to your face?"

"Oh, Bailey, please don't start."

"We need to start."

"Not now, Bailey. I'm still your mother. Now is *not* the time."

"Fine. How's the staging business?"

"Good. I'm decorating—well, not right now—five different houses. They are such beautiful houses. It makes the job a lot easier. Sometimes I bring Kat."

"Oh, yeah. She does. It's kind of cool," Kat said.

"Mom, how much longer do you have to be in here?"

"My doctor says I can go home on Sunday maybe, if I'm good."

"Good. I plan to be home until Tuesday, or later if I need to. I'll be here to help you settle home."

"Baby, I don't want you missing any classes because of me and my stupidity."

"Mom, we're not getting into it, remember?"

"Goodness. Katie, dear, can you go ask the nurse for a bucket of ice? Thank you."

"Sure, Mom."

"Bailey, come here." His mother patted the bed beside her fragile frame.

"Mom, I just can't stand…"

"Shh. I want you to forgive your father."

"No."

"Please, for me."

"Mom, you know that I love you, more than anything in this world; you and Kat. But don't ask me to look at that man and let go of the things that he's done to all of us."

"If you don't let go, you will carry them with you for the rest of your life."

"I already carry it around with me."

She put her broken hand up to his cheek. "My baby boy growing up. I know it is hard to control. You just remember that you are a good man and a kind person."

"Yes, ma'am." Kat clunked her way into the room with an overflowing bucket of ice. She placed it on the bedside table then sat down to gape at the mindless television show. "Can I run home and take a shower? I'll come back for Kat in about an hour or so."

"Oh, that's okay. Your father will be by later."

"Dad's coming?"

"Yes, he's bringing me a real dinner."

"Oh. Okay. Well, do you need anything before I head out? I'll come back later. It's good to see you." He almost swallowed that last statement. Her damaged face would haunt him for days.

"You get cleaned up, and come join us for dinner. Maybe you can ride over with your father and save on gas."

"Maybe. Bye." Bailey leaned down to kiss his mother on her forehead, waved to Kat, and walked out. Why did he leave so suddenly? He'd gone days, maybe even a week, before without showering, so why all of a sudden was a shower so important? He had nothing left to say to his mother. He didn't know how to look at her and come up with easy conversation. A small part of him probably wondered if his father was still at work. He needed to sort out in his mind, figure out what exactly he could do while he was home. Should he be a bystander, a protective son, or should he seek justice or revenge?

When he reached his car, he programmed his iPod to send Linkin Park to his radio. Bailey felt as if his life was whirling out of control. He saw himself as an imposter in his own family. He envied Kat's youthful ambivalence.

Bailey pulled into the driveway and sat for a minute or two, staring at his parents' house. He had lived in the three-story house since he was five. He had so many good memories here, but so many bad ones, too. He got out, pulled his overnight bag from the car trunk, and walked to the garage door to enter the code. After his parents installed the key code, he'd never bothered to get a front door key. Sometimes, though, the code wouldn't work. Today would be a gamble, in more ways than one.

It worked. The door slid open. Then the inside door to the house opened before he'd crossed the floor halfway. Bailey's father stood silhouetted by the kitchen light. He wasn't at work.

"My boy!" Mr. Johnson paced forward, closing the gap between him and his son. He embraced Bailey, and because his hands were full, Bailey could not return the enthusiastic hug.

"Dad."

"Is that all you have to say to me after being gone for months at school? What kinds of things have you learned?"

"Lots. And I have much to say to you. I need a shower first. I need to get settled, and then we are bringing Mom some real dinner."

"Oh, yeah. That. Did she say what she wanted?"

*A divorce from you.* "No."

"Then we'll bring her Mexican. I've been craving it all week, and no one has been here to cook. It's a lonely house what with Kat out all the time."

*And your battered wife in the hospital.* "She's allergic to peppers."

"Think I forgot?"

"Yes."

"Go get cleaned up. We'll leave when you're ready."

Bailey pushed by his father, focusing all of his tension in his fists and not in his dad's face. What a bastard to make jokes about no one to cook for him. Bailey headed up the stairs to his room. The house was a mess. He assumed his father did nothing while home, and Kat, from the sound of it, was out all the time. She had mentioned a boyfriend. Mission one: clean house for Mom before she comes home. Bailey threw his bag on the bed. His room looked the same as the day he'd left, just like his mother liked it.

He stripped down to his boxers and went to the hall bathroom. He almost got into the tub and started the spray when he remembered to grab a towel out of the hall closet. A long hot shower would help him relax.

---

*Bailey crouched outside his parents' bedroom door to listen. The yelling had stopped. The crashing and banging had also stopped. Now all he heard was quiet murmuring. As he strained to listen, Bailey sat on the floor and rested his head against the wall.*

*"I'm so sorry, baby."*

*"I know."*

*"Does it hurt too bad?"*

*"Only a little."*

*"You know you shouldn't do that. You should have remembered that I would react that way."*

*"I know."*

*"I'm sorry I had to remind you that you shouldn't hang my shirts until you iron them. Otherwise I go to work with*

*wrinkles, especially the collar. How can I properly represent my family at work if I have a crinkly shirt?"*

*"I'm sorry, Gregory. I was busy today. I had to drive Katie to the doctor so she could get a physical. She wants to try out for the soccer team in the spring."*

*"That's nice that she wants to do that. But you should have ironed my shirts before you left."*

*"I know. I forgot."*

*Bailey wanted to break into their room. What bullshit! Their last fight had been over his father's steak being cooked too well done. The one before that he had claimed that she purposely spent too much money repairing the dishwasher.*

*"Just don't forget next time, and I won't have to reprimand you."*

*"I'll try to be better."*

*"That's all I ever ask of you."*

*"Gregory, I need to go visit my mother next weekend."*

*"Why? Has the old hag finally croaked?"*

*"Goodness, no. She needs me to go over her finances. My father needs another prescription for his diabetes. They can afford it, but they'll have to redo their current budget."*

*"As long as it isn't Saturday. My boss is throwing an*

*afternoon party, and we must go and impress. I want you to wear that white dress."*

*"It has a stain in it, and it's much too cold for that thin material."*

*"Take care of the stain. And you can wear a shawl."*

*"Yes, of course I can. I know just the thing."*

———◇———

Bailey turned off the water. He wrapped a towel around his waist and ran a hand through his soaking wet hair. As he entered his room, he almost pissed himself. His father was sitting on his bed next to his overnight bag. The bag was open. From years of experience, Bailey knew his father was trying to provoke a fight over privacy. It wasn't going to happen.

"So I say we drive out a bit to that El Burrito place Mom likes," Bailey said.

"Sure, whatever."

"And we should order a couple chicken quesadillas and maybe a few enchiladas because they are her favorite."

"Okay."

"Also, we'll have to figure out a way to sneak it in because I'm sure the nurses won't allow such delicacies at the hospital."

"Why all the talk about your mother?"

"Why not, Dad? I'm here for her. Make no mistake about that."

"Are you challenging me?"

"No, of course not. But understand I'm not a naïve boy anymore who can easily forget Mommy's bruises with Daddy's great adventure stories. I know what you did, then and now. Don't even try to deny it."

"You…"

"No, not now. We have to get dinner and go see Mom and pick up Katie. *You* have to leave my room so I can change."

Empowered, Bailey watched as his bewildered father left his room. Mr. Johnson stared down the hallway as if he didn't know what to do. Just for effect, Bailey slammed the bedroom door, almost clipping his father's heels. He quickly dressed in casual jeans and a button-down red shirt and grabbed his wallet from his bag to put in his pocket: wallet, keys, phone, good. He opened the door again and ran down the stairs.

"Let's go, Dad! I'll be in the car."

Naturally, the bastard took his dear old time; he was not one to take orders. Ten minutes did the trick.

To avoid stewing in his car, Bailey turned on the radio and jammed out to Rage Against the Machine. The band was usually too hard rock for his tastes, but his father would dread every breathing moment. Was his behavior childish or deviant?

"Turn that shit off."

"What? I can't hear you."

"Little shit."

Bailey warmed on the inside. He would at least have fun while he was home. If he pushed his father too far, that far, he would and could fight back. At that moment, Jasmine's voice came back to him. *Fight him with words*, she had said before he left town. His mother was right when she said that now is not the time.

After getting food and a giant gift bag to hide it in, Bailey and his father went to the hospital room. Bailey noted with bemusement that, after one trip, he already knew the hallways better than his father. This spoke of how often he came to visit, and how often he made empty promises.

"We're back!"

"Bailey, so soon? Hello, Gregory."

"Sara. How are you feeling?"

"Good, now that my son has come home to see me. They say I can go home on Sunday."

"Fine. That's fine."

"Mom, we snuck in some food for you. Catch a whiff of this." Bailey got as close to her bed as he could and lowered the gift bag so she could smell.

"Oh, you know how to treat me, my baby."

"You're welcome. Kat, Jesus, come away from Barney for a second and eat some dinner." His sister rolled her eyes at him, but she turned off the television.

Bailey set the gift bag on the bedside table and shut the door and curtain. He almost reopened it again because the four of them seemed so tight it was suffocating. But if they wanted to eat a complete meal, they needed privacy from the nursing staff. Bailey handed everyone their dishes.

"We don't have plates, or forks, or anything," Mr. Johnson said. "How uncivilized."

"Dad, chill out. I'll run down to the cafeteria. In the meantime, use your fingers." Bailey strolled by the nurse's station and then bolted to the elevator. He waited a full second, and when it looked like it would take a while, he made for the stairs. He had energy to burn anyway. He skidded to a halt when he saw the gate to the entrance. Dammit. A young woman in a candy striper outfit walked by.

"Hey!" Bailey called.

She whirled around, startled by the stranger.

"Hi, I don't need to get any food, but I was wondering if you could hand me three forks? Four! Sorry, four forks."

"All meal trays are supplied with proper utensils." She passed him forks through the gate. He returned her favor with a dashing smile and ran away, yelling, "Thanks!"

He took the stairs back up two at a time the first three flights. Then he had to slow down because he was out of breath; he really needed to get back in shape. Maybe he'd run tomorrow morning. That would be a good release of energy.

"Here we go," he announced himself to silence. His whole family sat staring at the black screen of the television, not touching their food. "Seriously, guys, you can eat now. I have forks."

"Good. Kat, find something good on television. Something we all can enjoy while we eat."

"Yeah, like a channel exists. Oh, that reminds me of a story this girl at school told me. She was fighting with her little brother over the TV remote, and she let go all of a sudden, and it flew back and smacked him in the face. He lost his two front teeth, and they weren't even baby teeth either. I feel so bad for that guy when he grows up. I mean, who would want to walk around with a huge gap in your smile? Geesh." The family passed the rest of the evening in awkward silence, especially after leaving the hospital.

Bailey woke early the next morning. Why? He wasn't sure. He could motivate himself to go running. He could go out for some breakfast ingredients and make everyone in the house a grand meal. He wandered downstairs in his plaid boxers, where he found Kat already at the kitchen table.

"What are you doing up this early, loser?"

"I stopped sleeping in this house years ago, Bailey. Have you already forgotten?"

"I'm sorry, Kat."

"Eh, whatever. What doesn't kill me will make me stronger. I always figured there should have been another line to that saying, though: It will, however, make you insane."

"Fair enough." Bailey sat next to her. So young and reading the weekend paper. "I worry about you sometimes, living here with no one to protect you."

"Bailey, how you underestimate me. I am my father's daughter."

"I'm afraid we both share that fate, taking after Dad."

"How do you mean?"

"I mean that I feel Dad's temper sometimes."

"Oh, duh. So do I."

"But sometimes I can't control it."

"Well, that sucks. Try harder?"

"Wow. Thanks, Kat. Want some breakfast?" Bailey got up to look in the refrigerator. His eyebrows went up when all he found was one egg, expired milk, and leftover hamburgers, which he assumed had been dinner about a week ago. "Damn, I'm going to have to go to the store."

"Oh! Grab me some tampons while you're there?"

"Yeah, sure thing! Over my dead body. You either come with me or wait until Mom comes home."

"I'll get dressed."

"Me, too."

# CHAPTER NINE

Kat

From the hallway, Kat could see her brother lying on his bed, nose buried in his iPad. She knocked.

"Come in. Don't linger in the doorway."

Of course he knew she was there. "Whatcha doin'?"

"Just doing FaceTime with Lina."

"Oh yeah, is she still there?"

"Nah, she signed off a few minutes ago."

"How is she?"

"She's good, I think."

"Good." Kat sat on the opposite side of the bed. She fiddled with the tie strings of her pajama bottoms.

"Why didn't you tell me, Katie," Bailey said, reverting to her childhood name.

"I did."

"Sooner."

"I don't know, Bail. What were you going to do, besides come home? I didn't want to drag you back here for something that won't change. I usually deal with it."

"You shouldn't have to deal with it. Are you okay?"

"I'm fine."

"Don't lie to me. I know how it is. You hanging in there?"

"Yeah, I'm doing okay. I stay busy."

"Why don't you come live with me?"

"Pssh, yeah. What, I'll hang out in your dorm room common area? I'll bet all of your male roommates will love that."

"No, I mean, I could get a place. Off campus."

"And then you could become my parent? No, thanks."

"Think about it."

"I will." Kat stood and walked over to the bookshelves in the corner that housed her old textbooks, scrapbooks, and achievement awards. "I can't just leave my life here. Sure, it sucks sometimes, but I'm a junior at school. I have my classes all planned, and I have friends."

"Yeah?"

"Don't sound so surprised. I'm trying."

"Tell me."

"Well, I've been hanging out with some art students, some classmates. I've been to a couple of parties."

"Were you drinking?"

"No," Kat said. Bailey held her gaze until she looked away. "Maybe a little."

"I bet they loved that," Bailey said, nodding at the master bedroom.

"They didn't find out. Flynn got me home okay."

"Flynn?"

"Yeah. He's a friend."

"Kat." Without saying more, Bailey demanded more information. The iPad sat forgotten on his lap.

"He's just a boy, Bail."

"I need his full name and license number."

"Stop. He's nice. He's good for me."

Bailey didn't respond. It was all or nothing when they talked about guys. Kat remembered her first boyfriend in grade school passing her a note that said, "Do you like me? Yes □ No □" She remembered Bailey walking her down the street to the boy's house after school when she wrote "I don't know" on a corner of the note and gave it back to him.

"Want to watch a movie?"

"On your iPad?"

"No, dweeb. On the massive 75-inch screen downstairs."

"But Dad."

"Dad isn't here."

Kat didn't ask. Honestly, she didn't care. "Okay. What do you want to watch?"

"The new *Bond* movie?"

"Heh, I sorta already saw that one, the other day, with…"

"Flynn? Okay, fine. Um, let's go old school. *Lethal Weapon* marathon."

"You're on! I'll make popcorn."

"Don't forget the chocolate and Skittles," he yelled as she ran from the room. How could she forget? Kat and her brother had always mixed popcorn with sweet candy; it was kind of gross but awesome at the same time. Kat thundered down the stairs and into the kitchen. She opened cabinets, threw bowls on the counter, and slid on her socks over to the pantry to grab the Orville's popcorn and Reese's Pieces, tossing the bags across the room to land on the counter near the bowls.

Several hours later, Kat and Bailey snuggled under separate blankets on the couch, the popcorn and candy deserted on the coffee table between their feet. With each movie, Kat slumped a little lower on the couch cushion, and Bailey smirked. He simply watched in silence as she finally let her head rest on her hand and her eyelids slowly closed. She had made it through three of the four movies. But she needed the sleep.

Bailey reached over and stuck his finger in her ear, making her jerk awake and give him the stink eye. "Go to bed, punk. You get an A for effort. We've got lots to do tomorrow."

Kat groaned as she pushed the blanket off. She slumped her way out of the room and toward the stairs to her bedroom, glancing back once at her brother. He waved her off. Before turning down the hallway to the stairwell, she said, "Goodnight...it's good to have you home."

One time when I was a little girl, I stayed up
very late after bedtime, lying on the couch
with Mom and Bailey. I was curled against
her warm body and her red bathrobe with
white clouds on it as she caressed her fingers
through my hair. Her fingernails against my
scalp made me sleepy. My brother sat beside
us. I can't remember what we were watching
on TV or anything significant about their
conversation. I just remember the warmth of
the side table lamp and the deep rumble of
my mother's voice through her chest. I tried
to stay awake, but I had never felt as safe
as I did that night in her arms.

"What are you doing here?" Kat had barely finished
her question before Flynn's lips touched hers, and he
gently pushed her back into the house with his body. He
knew her brother was in town, and he'd given her about
a day of peace.

"I wanted to see you," he said.

"But…"

Flynn kissed Kat again, pushing her back farther until she backed up against the hall closet door.

"Hmm," she moaned in response as he deepened the kiss and brought a hand up to caress her cheek, her neck, into her hair. She relaxed into his body. Kat's arms came up to rest on his shoulders, half pushing him away, half pulling him closer. Her legs coiled around his hip bone, and Flynn groaned into her mouth. They pulled from each other's strength. There was no plan beyond their tangling tongues, their mixed breath, their urgency to fill a void within one another.

Under Flynn's leather jacket, Kat balled her fist into Flynn's shirt. She heard a muffled cough. Huh? Oh shit. She couldn't warn Flynn. Kat's head whipped to the side to see Bailey watching them from the base of the stairs, one eyebrow cocked up and a dimple deepened into a smirk. "Bail, this is…" Flynn was still trying to nuzzle her neck. Kat gave two solid pushes against his chest.

"But babe…"

"Flynn. This is my brother, Bailey."

Flynn's hands dropped from her hips immediately. He stepped away from Kat.

"Hey, what's up man?" Kat realized Flynn couldn't look her brother in the eye. Who knows where his hands had been? All he could remember was the soft warm flesh of her butt under those tight jeans. God, he wiped his palms on his own pants and forced his gaze upward. "Kat has told me a lot about you. It's nice to meet you."

"Has she?" Bailey's grip on the stair railing tightened, and his gaze transferred from Flynn back to Kat. They were both slightly out of breath and disheveled.

"She tells me you go to school in Charleston," Flynn said. "That's a really cool town."

"Yeah, it's neat."

"Bailey." Kat shot a stern look toward her brother. Why would she have thought he'd be civil, friendly even?

Flynn continued, "I'm due at the Virginia Beach police station in a couple weeks. I just finished my training a few months ago. Before I met Kat."

"So you'll just leave her here when you have to go? Use her and lose her?"

"Bailey!"

"Never mind. Good luck to you," Bailey said, dismissing Flynn. "Kat, we have some things to get ready for when Mom comes home tomorrow."

"I know. Just give me a minute?"

Bailey didn't move. He stared at the couple as though Flynn would disappear and their conversation would come to an end. "A minute, Bail. Please," Kat said as she set her hand on Flynn's chest, signaling for him to stay there.

To get by them, Bailey came down the remaining steps and crossed the landing, sizing up Flynn as he walked toward the kitchen.

"Wow, what a douche."

"Flynn, he's not. He's just protective."

"A protective douche."

"Stop saying that. He's not. He just doesn't trust people. You don't understand."

"I'm getting a little tired of you saying that to me."

"Please, let's not fight."

"We're not fighting. We're talking." Flynn watched as Kat's face turned stony. She removed her hand from his chest and stepped away from him. "Kat?"

"I think you should go, Flynn. I'm busy here. My mom comes home tomorrow, and we have lots to do to get the house ready."

"Don't do that," Flynn almost whispered. "Don't pull away from me. I can feel it; I can see it in your eyes. Don't shut down on me. I'm sorry. God, Kat, you have so many triggers, and I'm still learning them all. But give me a break. I just wanted to see you. I missed you."

Kat nodded, but her eyes remained distant. She wrapped her arms around herself. "I…"

"Yeah, I know. But I do understand, Kat. You are like a virus spreading underneath my skin, and I don't know whether to scratch at it, soothe it with lotion, or cut it out."

"I'm like a virus?"

"That didn't come out right. You can't tell me that you don't feel it, too." He took a hesitant step toward her. "That you can't feel my body heat as much as if I were another limb."

"No, you're wrong. It's called sex."

"Okay, yeah, that's a part of it. But I feel this force drawing me to you. It's not just physical. It's mental. Like my mind reaches for yours, to see what you're thinking. Because I never know. Sometimes when your guard is down, I get a glimpse, but bam, your walls go back up before I get a clear picture."

"You're leaving."

"Not for a couple weeks."

"You're still leaving. It's best if we don't get involved."

"Don't start anything because it will end. Okay, for now. We're not done talking about this. I'll be back. Go do your stuff for your mom. Call me later if you want."

Kat stayed where she was with her arms still crossed as Flynn left the house. He was right. She did feel it, probably more so than he did. But she had more practice keeping herself at a distance, keeping herself safe.

In the kitchen, Kat found Bailey at the table drinking from a mug. He asked, "Want some hot chocolate?"

"You were an ass."

"He's leaving."

Kat wanted to argue, out of spite, but Bailey was right. She turned to the pantry to get the chocolate pouch before Bailey could see her eyes start to shine. Hadn't she learned enough not to let her guard down?

I have a photograph of me with my father where I am maybe two or three. I'm in a purple snowsuit, with a matching bonnet, my fine baby auburn hair peeking out beneath. My little hand in his, we stand with our backs to the camera, looking out over the yard. A few feet of snow fell that winter. He is looking down at me; I guess we're about to take the first step into that snow, and he's checking to see if I'm ready. You can see my little face upturned to his, tilted away from the camera still, but eager to return his gaze. I'm sure if you could fast forward a photograph, you would see that first step, his much larger than my own. And as the snow came up over my waist, maybe he picked me up. Maybe he carried me through the snow instead of letting me struggle through it with my little legs. Maybe, with me secure in his arms, he turned to the camera and gave a great, momentous smile for my mother, behind the lens. Just maybe...

"Why do you think she never left?" Kat offered the question as she and Bailey rearranged furniture in the den to make a temporary bedroom in preparation for their mother's return from the hospital. With her broken ribs, she wouldn't be able to walk up the stairs easily, and the chaise longue chair would serve well enough as a bed, for a night or two anyway.

"Left him?"

"Yeah."

"I don't know. I have theories."

"Which are?"

"Well, the only one that really matters is that she loves him."

"That's messed up."

"I didn't say it made sense."

"I always thought she was stronger than that."

"Stronger than what? Love?"

"No, I mean, strong enough to know what he was doing to her and know that she deserved better."

"Mom's not weak, Kat. You might have been too young to remember, but she's tough. She's tough with us."

"That's different."

"No, it isn't. It's how she copes. As for why she never left, she tried to several times, that I can remember.

Maybe in the beginning she stayed for us, or she stayed because she thought it would change. But she stays now because they've come to need each other."

"Then why do you always try to come in and break them up? You are always trying to get her to leave him."

"Just because this is what they want doesn't mean it's healthy. Maybe she thinks that leaving is lonelier than staying. But I'd rather live every day of the rest of my life alone than put up with this shit."

"Is it me?"

"What?"

"Does she stay because of me?" Bailey stopped folding the clean laundry. Kat had paused from dusting the bookshelves to glance back at him.

"Maybe. But, Kat, I learned long ago that it's her choice. Forcing her to see the truth or change her mind only makes her stick her feet in harder. They are alike in that way. Stubborn."

"How the hell did they ever end up together?"

"It wasn't like this in the beginning; I'd bet money on it. You know their laugh? When they hug? Or that look she gets when she's teasing him, when it's good for a while?"

Kat felt goose bumps rush up her arms. She knew those times well. She didn't trust them.

"Yeah, they make my skin crawl, too, because we aren't used to it," Bailey continued. "But back in the day, I bet it was more of that than him yelling at her. By the stories she used to tell, it was like any other fledgling romance."

"I can't imagine."

"Sure you can. I just saw it with you and Flynn in the hallway this morning. Sometimes love turns sour." Kat turned away again to keep dusting. "But Kat, sometimes love doesn't turn sour."

It was a lame attempt at a peace offering, and she knew him too well to think he believed it. Still, deep down, maybe Bailey wanted a little hope, too. Everyone needs a little hope in humanity. Otherwise, what was the point?

"Have you found love before?" Kat waited. It seemed as if he wouldn't respond, but she heard his exhale. "Do you love Lina?"

"I love Lina, but not in the way you think. Lina and I love each other based on trust, respect, and friendship."

"How romantic."

"It might not be pretty, but Lina and I will be friends forever. Period. I don't question it. But it's not romantic with us. I'd rather know that she'll be there for me when I need her and know that I'll be there for her when she really needs me."

"You need each other."

"Yes. But it's bigger than that. It's not all serious. It's hard to explain, but she reminds me of a version of myself. When I want to remember that version, I call her up. You remember when she and I used to take those art lessons together at Valerie's gallery?"

"Yeah, that crazy lady with the goats."

"Well, I don't paint anymore. But sometimes when I'm walking alone at night or driving down the road and I get this urge to pick up a brush, that's Lina. That's Lina reminding me of something we used to share. She reminds me of a better time. A time full of potential. And I remind her of stuff, too."

"Like what?"

"I don't know. Um, once she told me that I represented home to her. That no matter how much time passed since we'd seen each other, all it took was one glance, and she felt safe, she felt home."

"I want that."

"You have it." Kat turned, and Bailey was standing beside her. "In me." Their hug was strained but heartfelt.

"Maybe Mom and Dad remind each other of that."

"Maybe. But at a certain point, it's called codependency. And you have to be careful whom you depend on. Except you never have to be careful with depending on me. I'm your big brother, and it is my job, my purpose to protect you."

Kat saw a flash of Hunter's face. And then Flynn's. "That may be the case, but Bail, you're leaving too."

He didn't respond at first. He brought the bulging laundry basket of folded clean clothes to the doorway to carry it upstairs. Then he spoke over his shoulder, "But I'm here now."

He hollered from the hallway, "Dishes next."

Kat had never spoken like that before with Bailey, about their parents, about life. She had always known that Lina was just a friend, but he'd never explained before. She wasn't even sure she fully understood. He probably didn't either. They were just kids, after all. They were just children trying to figure out their place in the world. It was hard to figure it all out, though, when they were living for other people. Kat lived for her mother. Her mother lived for her father. Bailey lived for Lina. Hunter had lived for his parents. Flynn lived for everyone else. But maybe that was the point. To live only for yourself could lead to a very lonely life. Perhaps the point to living, and in some cases dying, was to leave an impact on others. A person's legacy rests in the ripples left on the lives of friends and family. Hadn't Hunter's death led Kat to that darkroom, which led her to meet Mel and go to that party, where she met Flynn?

# CHAPTER TEN

## Bailey

Bailey parked the car in the driveway and got out to help his mother. She was home. He ran to the passenger side, opened her door, and crouched down so she could wrap an arm around his shoulders. He gradually stood straight as she maneuvered out of the car. When they were both upright, he paused.

"How are you, okay?"

"Just dandy. I'm out of the car, aren't I?

Fine. Let me just take a break on the couch first for a while. You can make me some lunch. I'm so tired of hospital food."

"Deal."

It took Bailey thirty minutes to get his mom up the five-stair stoop to the front door. After each step, they had to stop, take a breath, and smell some flowers, or so he pretended when she began wheezing.

"Bailey, you are such a good son."

"Ha, just remember that next time you want to harp on me about grades and girlfriends, okay?"

"Deal."

"So you want a sandwich? Turkey? Provolone? Rye bread?"

"Yes, sounds great."

"Alright, almost there. Are you ready?"

"I can do it."

He used his body to support her while his hands unlocked the door. Hopefully, Kat was just inside finishing the cleaning he'd demanded of her earlier. He pushed the door ajar and came back to his mother. He practically lifted her over the threshold, but he couldn't squeeze her too hard because he discovered that sore spots lined her ribs.

"Kat, we're home." Bailey looked up the stairs and saw his sister run down the hall to her room with a bundle of folded clothes.

"Mom!" Kat came down the stairs to take over duties.

"Put her on the couch for now. I'm going to get her bags and then make some lunch. Want some?"

"Sure, sounds good."

"Good."

Bailey went back outside and welcomed the new freedom in his limbs. His mother wasn't heavy, but he had supported her whole weight. He grabbed her bag from the back seat, and as he locked the car, Kat came out of the house.

"How is she?" Kat asked.

"Why don't you ask her?"

"I did. Now give me the real answer."

"She's fragile. Doctor says about two weeks before she's completely back to normal."

"Wow. Two weeks."

"Yeah. I don't think I can miss that much school, Kat. You'll have to be here to watch him."

"Him?"

"Yes, I mean Dad."

"What can I do to stop him?"

"I didn't ask you to stop him. I asked you to watch out for her, okay?"

"Alright."

"Call me the second anything else happens. I'll be home for another day or so. And the house looks good. Thank you."

"No problem. It was moderately empowering to do the chores because I chose to, not because someone was barking at me to do them."

"Welcome to adulthood. Want to help me cook?"

"No? Geesh."

Bailey smiled. Some things would never change. He went back into the house to check on his mother. Kat had settled her so she could lie down and watch television.

"Where's your father?"

"I don't know."

"Bailey."

"I told him I was going to pick you up, and he mumbled something about golf or work."

"Hand me the phone."

He ignored her request. "Lunch in ten minutes."

Looking in the refrigerator no longer made him grimace. He had gone to the store and filled the fridge with fresh fruits and veggies as well as stocked the freezer with a few frozen pizzas for his sister. If or when she ate, the meal was never balanced. Bailey's pocket vibrated. He spun the bread bag closed, opened his phone, and rested it between his shoulder and his head.

"Lina, hang on a sec."

"Okay."

"Here you go, Mom."

"Thank you, baby. You are so sweet. Who's on the phone?"

"Lina. Katie! Food! Alright, Lin, what's up?"

"I'm just calling to see what's new in hell. I mean, what it's like being home."

"Yeah, so far it's been bundles of fun mixed with fields of daisies. I almost can't contain my happiness."

"Damn, and I didn't come home why?"

"No, I still don't think you should have come. My mom just came home today."

"How bad?"

"Bad."

"How bad?"

"Lin, do you remember that time in ninth grade when I didn't come to school for a week?"

"Oh God. That bad really?"

"Yeah. I don't know what to do other than be here to defend her since she can't."

"Damn. Good luck. Call me if you need anything, especially just to talk."

"Will do, baby girl. What's new with you?"

"Not much. Same old. I have a paper due Wednesday and Thursday this week."

"I'm sorry. You decided to be an English major."

"Yep. Silly love of the written word and all that."

"I know you can do it. Just keep it up."

"Thanks, Bail. So are *you* okay with all this?"

"Sure. I don't have a choice. It's my job to protect my family."

"What happens when you get into a fight with your dad?"

"I won't get in a fight with my dad."

"Bailey, I know you better than that. I know that ever since you developed hair on your chest, you've wanted to show your father what kind of man you are."

"But I don't want to show him that I am the same man as him."

"Fair enough."

"Lin, I got to go. I'll call you in a few days on my way back down to school. We'll have seven hours to talk then."

"Okay, take care, Bail."

"You, too."

Bailey leaned against the kitchen counter. His sandwich was already on the kitchen table, but he'd lost his appetite. He gazed out the window over the sink as a neighbor's car drove down the street. Just as he snapped out of his reverie, remembering to check on his mother and sister, his father's car pulled into the driveway.

Mr. Johnson got out of his car carrying his coat and briefcase. Halfway to the door, he stopped suddenly and turned back. From the back seat, he pulled a bouquet of flowers: red lilies. Dammit, his mother's favorite. That sole gesture from him would make her coo and gush about him for a week. In the house, Mr. Johnson set his case by the closet and his coat on the hook then went straight to the living room as if he knew just where his wife would be.

"Hey, sweetheart."

"Oh, Gregory, they are beautiful!"

"I'm sorry I couldn't be here to bring you home. I had a last-minute work meeting."

"It's alright. Bailey was all I needed to get home and settled. He even told Katie to clean the house. Isn't it nice?"

"I see that. How are you feeling?"

"I'm fine now. I just had some lunch."

"Good. I was thinking if you are up to it, we could go out to that nice Italian restaurant tonight."

"I don't think that is such a good idea, Dad." Bailey stepped into the room behind his father.

"I wasn't asking you, Bailey."

"Well, since you weren't there to listen to her doctor's final orders, I'll fill you in. He said bed rest and minimal movement for at least three days."

"It's just dinner, son."

"It took me half an hour to get her in the house from the driveway. Do you think you can just take her out to dinner?"

"I can do whatever I want."

"Fine. But have you asked her?"

"What do you say, dear?"

"I don't know, Gregory."

"Mom, just remember how hard it was to get in the house."

"Yes. Maybe we can go some other night when I have more strength."

"That's fine. I'm going to go upstairs and work some more then."

"No, stay. We can watch a movie together or something."

"Waste of time. Watch one with Bailey, since he seems to be the only thing you need."

"Gregory."

"Mom, let him go," Bailey said as his father turned and left.

"I don't understand," his mother said quietly. "There must be something wrong."

"The only thing that plagues his mind is the fact that I'm here blocking every step of his power play."

"What did I tell you in the hospital, Bailey?"

"And I told you no. I'm too old and too tired of playing your games. You chose this life; I didn't."

"I didn't choose *this* life, though."

"You chose the man."

"Bailey, when are you going to forgive *me* for this marriage?"

"I don't blame you, Mom."

"You blame me for not leaving."

"I just don't understand why you never did."

"He's my husband. I love him. And twenty-five years ago, I said vows: till death do us part."

"That death should not be by his hand."

"I am stronger than you think."

"My point is you shouldn't have to be."

"Let's watch a movie. I miss you, baby. I don't want to spend the whole weekend fighting."

"Okay, Mom. What should we watch?"

---

*"Come on, Mom. We're going to be late."*

*"I'm coming! Start the car!"*

*"Okay!"*

*Bailey went outside and started the car to defrost the windows. It was winter break, his father had journeyed into work, and Katie was down the street at a sleepover. Without any more distractions, they could enjoy the wintry afternoon together. His mother burst from the house, locked the front door, and made her way to the car through the thick layer of snow that had settled on the ground.*

*"Alright, I'm ready!" she exclaimed as she buckled her seat belt.*

*"Awesome. I'm so excited about seeing this movie."*

*"Do you think the theater will be closed?"*

*"Not if they can help it."*

*"Drive carefully."*

*"Mom."*

*"I know, I know. You're a delivery boy for Dominoes. But I'm still your mother."*

*"What are you going to do when I leave for college in the fall?"*

*"Bug Katie?" They both fell into fits of laughter imagining her response: "Like geesh, Mom. Seriously not cool."*

*"Really, Mom, are you going to be okay when I leave?"*

*"Of course, baby. What makes you say that?"*

*"The bruise on your wrist." Instinctively, she pulled her shirt down farther over the mark. "It's not the first I've noticed either."*

"I'll be fine. I have your sister to keep me company. What matters to me is that you go to school and get an education."

"I will, Mom. But I still worry about being so far away from you and Kat."

"Tell you what. I'll call you the moment I need you to come home."

"Can you make that seven hours before you need me just so I can have time to drive home?"

"Sure thing, sweetie."

"Here I come, icy roads and warm movie theater."

"I feel like I'm a kid again playing hooky from school."

"Mom! Did you really have to go to school when the roads were like this?"

"Yes, and worse. But don't tell Katie about me skipping school; it will give her ideas."

"Aren't you worried about me skipping school?"

"First off, you are my dependable, honest Bailey. Second, you only have one more semester before going away to school. You deserve a break before you go off to college."

"Wow, Mom. You are on a roll tonight. Is college really hell?"

*"I was an English major. All I ever did was read great literature and write massive paper after paper. With your interest in history and religion, you'll take more tests. I was not one to memorize facts; you are."*

*"Tests versus papers—I'm honestly not sure which one is better."*

*"You'll find out once you get settled into your classes and learn which professors are better to take for which classes."*

*"Mom, you are so cool."* She tipped her head back and laughed, letting go in a way Bailey had rarely heard. *He liked seeing her like this, especially right before he was leaving her. He would hold onto this image of her forever.*

Bailey finished wiping down the kitchen counters. His mother was upstairs taking a nap; she'd only agreed after he promised to do the laundry and empty the dishwasher. Katie was at the mall with her friend Mel.

Mr. Johnson walked into the house before Bailey could think to escape to another room. Here it comes. His dad put his briefcase and coat by the door as he always did, then made his way into the kitchen, looking for someone to hear his complaints. Mr. Johnson coughed to announce himself.

"So what did you do today?"

"Not much. Got Mom settled, helped Katie finish cleaning, and thinking about what to grab for dinner since everyone else ate earlier."

"What about me? Didn't you make anything?"

"How was I supposed to know when you were coming home? If you were coming home?"

"What is that supposed to mean?"

"That means I wasn't going to cook a meal without knowing whether you would work late or if you would come home at all."

"You said if."

"Yes I did."

"Why wouldn't I come home?"

"Sorry, I was just projecting my own hopes and dreams."

"Since you came home, you have been giving me attitude. Well, it's going to stop right now!"

"Or what, Dad? You going to hit me? That would be a change."

"Don't you talk back to me, boy!"

"I'm not a boy anymore. I don't know if you can

tell, but I am a full-grown man now, and I look a lot like you."

"You're not a man yet, even if you aren't a boy anymore."

"Dad, you don't know what you're talking about."

"I should teach you a lesson for questioning my authority."

"Authority? Teach me a lesson? Is that what you did to Mom so she ended up in the hospital?"

"Your mother was not in the hospital because of me."

"It amazes me that you believe your own lies."

"I'm not lying, Bailey. Your mother was sick beyond my help. She needed constant care that I just couldn't give her."

"Because every time you touch her, she bruises. Is her skin really that sensitive? Or is maybe your touch a little rougher than you think?"

"Our relationship is none of your business."

"Yeah, sure. She's my mother, one of the most amazing women I know, especially for staying here with your sorry ass all these years."

"That's it." Mr. Johnson tried to grab Bailey by the collar. Bailey dodged the grasp and ran into the living room; he didn't want to fight. "Don't run away from me!"

"I'm not running away from you, you bastard. I am not fighting you!"

"If you say you are a man, face me as one."

"I don't have to be a man to face you. I am a man because I can walk away."

"What sense does that make?"

"A kind of sense that you will never understand. You establish control through your fists. I will establish control with my restraint."

"That's bullshit!"

"Bailey!" His mother screamed from the bedroom upstairs. "Bailey! Stop!"

"It's okay, Mom! We're not fighting. Go back to sleep."

"She was sleeping? Nice going."

"You are such an asshole. I wish you had stayed at work. Maybe you can go back and come home after I've left. I'll be gone tomorrow morning."

"This is my home."

"Well, you sure have a hell of a way of making everyone feel at home here. You hit Mom, and I bet you yell at Katie when she fails to meet your unreasonable expectations."

"I push your sister to be better. Those damn teenybopper kids she hangs with influence her to do bad things."

"Jesus, Dad. Are you that out of touch with reality that you don't see that Katie is a teenybopper? There is nothing wrong with that; it's a phase! Do you remember being a teenager, or were you even one to begin with?"

"Teenagers back when I was young are not the same as today's teenagers. They do drugs! They have sex! They skip school!"

"Like you didn't do any of those things!"

"Bailey! Stop!" His mother screamed again.

"I never did the things these kids do."

"Whatever. I'll pretend that I believe you. That doesn't change the fact that you beat your wife." Mr. Johnson reached out and slapped Bailey across the face. "And your son."

"You deserved that."

"Just like mom deserved it every time, too?"

"I don't know what you're talking about."

"You ever notice how she sometimes has bruises all over her body or how right now she can barely get herself out of bed?"

"Your mother feels ill at times, and she stumbles a lot."

"You almost had me fooled."

"Don't be smart."

"No, Dad. That's the thing. I am smart. I hear you yelling at night. I hear the sound of your fist making contact with her cheekbone; it's like a crack. I hear her— what you call—stumbling because you push her to the ground. And then I hear her stay up all night crying, wondering how the man she married could be such a monster."

"I don't do any of these things! It sounds like you have issues that you need help with. Perhaps you should seek professional guidance."

"You aren't hearing me. You have control issues. You belittle me, and Mom, and even Katie with your words," Bailey massaged his throbbing cheek. "And with your hands. You are not a man if you need to beat your family into submission. A real man brings his wife flowers, but not after he puts her in the hospital. A real man touches his wife gently and with respect. A real man can look at his son and recognize the potential in him, not the wasted talents."

Halfway through Bailey's speech, Bailey's father looked away, his eyes filling with that all-too-familiar rage. Knowing he would avoid his bedroom if Bailey retreated there first, he brushed past him quickly and started up the stairs. "Mom!"

Bailey stood in the doorway. His mother was sitting on the floor, leaning against the bed. Apparently, she had attempted to get up but she was too weak. How often she puts herself in danger's way to protect her children, Bailey thought. When he was younger, he'd let her, not understanding the impact of that courage and love. Now that he could defend himself, he would take on all of her fights.

"Bailey," she whispered. She looked up with a helpless gaze; how could his father not see that look every time he raised his hand or pushed her aside? Bailey helped his mother back into bed. He hesitated at the door and changed his mind about leaving. He gently lay next to her on the bed, and they faced each other.

"Mom…"

She placed her broken hand on his enflamed cheek. Bailey felt as if his eyes also shone with helplessness. In the end, though, he knew he would get to leave the house. His mother would forever stay. He remembered when he used to plead with her to leave, or he'd take advantage of each hesitation after uttering the word "divorce." She never followed through, so he gave up. Then he pledged never to stay in a marriage that no longer benefited himself or his wife. What possible kind of love could she feel for his father to make her stay?

"Mom, I love you."

Her eyes welled up with tears.

"I love you so much, baby."

"I'm twenty-one years old."

"You will always be my baby. And you're lying on my bed like you used to as a small boy."

"I was remembering how it felt to be a kid. Then I realized that it was so long ago before Katie was born.

When he threw you down the stairs seven months pregnant...I wish that I had been older so I could have stopped him."

"It wasn't your place to protect me, Bailey. Katie is fine anyway."

"It might not have been my place, but you're my mother. What son wouldn't feel protective when her life is in danger?"

"It was my baby's life that was in danger."

"Even so."

"Oh, we always talk about the same things. How are you? Aren't there any girls at school you're interested in?"

"Let me tell you about Jasmine," he sighed, letting the topic drop for once.

"Ooh, goodie. Love stories, my favorite."

# CHAPTER ELEVEN

*Kat*

Kat jumped up on the oversized tire in the children's playground as Flynn ran around the course at Nike Park. She watched him move. He was a good runner, his form fluid yet quick. He circled back toward her, slowing to a walk as he stepped onto the pebble base under the playground.

"Hey there," he said. "Do you come here often?"

"Sometimes, with strange men."

"Oh yeah? Who are these strange men? Do they take advantage of you?"

"Yes, I give them all sex."

"Well then. When can this guy get in on that action?"

"Oh, I'm sorry, I'm quite exhausted today. Perhaps later?" Kat tilted her head as he stepped up to her and leaned on the tire. His hands rested on her thighs, and he smiled up at her, squinting to see her face in the midday sunlight. "You need sunglasses."

"I don't like to wear them when I run."

"Makes sense. So, what else must be done, workout boy?"

"I need to work my arms a bit. I could use you as a bench press bar."

"Yeah, that's a no. There's a high bar over there. Why don't you go do some pull-ups."

"Good compromise. You good here?"

"Yup. I brought a book. Go be buff and strong."

"And then we'll go back to my house?"

"Sure, but you stink."

"Yes, I will have to shower. You can hang out, snoop around, look at all the baby pictures of Mel and me on the walls."

"Sweet. Some dreams do come true." Kat smiled down at Flynn, nudging his shoulder away to encourage him to finish his workout. She wasn't sure why she had tagged along. He had called and asked her to hang out today, and he'd shown up in sweats. But she didn't really mind. It was better than staying at home.

At the high bar, Flynn easily did ten pull-ups. Back on the ground, he swung his arms across his chest and out away from his body. Then he did ten more. He completed one more set and then returned to Kat by doing cartwheels all the way to the tire. Her giggles echoed across the park.

"Let's go, babe." Flynn grabbed Kat's hand to help her off the tire. Sure, his hand was sweaty, but touching his skin electrified her. She had never felt such a strong connection to another person, let alone one of the opposite sex. She liked it. A lot. She was tired of closing herself off from other people. She didn't have to share all of the gory details of her life; she wanted to share in the good times, too. She needed a balance to all of the bad stuff that was beyond her control. A person could lose faith in everything if they didn't have some kind of positivity.

Kat recognized Flynn's house when they pulled into the driveway. Before she could ask, he said, "Everyone is gone for the day."

"Oh, okay." Should she be nervous? Was he hoping for something to happen? She had only been joking earlier in the park, but he was older. Maybe he expected her to…no, he was a good guy, a patient guy. At least she hoped so. It was a far cry from holding hands to a home run.

"Alright, I'm going to go grab a quick shower. You know where most everything is, so make yourself at home. I'll find you when I'm done."

Kat nodded. She stood where she was until he was out of sight and then circled around the main foyer. Where to start? He was right; there were photos everywhere. It was so strange how simple photographs could turn a house into a home. The pictures gave the rooms personality and smiles. They gave it a history. Of course, it's always the good memories that make the scrapbook. No one sees the bad times documented—except in police reports.

Living in the past could be dangerous, though. Already Kat was reviewing college brochures and listening to "decide your future" lectures from teachers. There were too many options. All she wanted was to get out of that house. She didn't care where she went or what she was doing. And sure, logically, while she understood concepts like supporting herself financially and following her passion, those goals seemed counterintuitive. She doubted her passion for photography and art would yield a large salary, if one at all. She had a lot to think about.

Kat wandered upstairs to Flynn's room. There were no surprises here: queen-sized bed with dark green rumpled sheets and bedspread, the red beanbag chair—*when was the last time he'd actually sat in it?*—clothes littering the floor, some clean, some not, and a small wooden desk where the TV sat, with its friends, the DVD player, Xbox, and Nintendo? Wow, old school. Had that been there last time?

She saw a pair of DJ headphones tossed to the side, still connected to an iPod on the desk. Kat picked them up and put them on. What was he listening to? She turned on the iPod and pushed play. Please be something good. She recognized the first few bars but couldn't immediately place them. The screen said "I Wish You Were Here" by Incubus.

Overly sentimental? Or maybe just romantic. Kat closed her eyes and let the song play on. She relaxed, imagining herself in a safe place. There was no school, no assignments, no conflicts, not today. After the song ended, Kat removed the headphones. A muffled sound behind her made her turn. Flynn stood in his bedroom doorway in a white towel, his dirty blonde hair still wet and flat against his head. But he was gorgeous. His lusty stare warmed her face.

"That cold shower didn't help."

"I'm sorry. I, uh, should leave so you can change."

"Well, that might be best."

"Yes, of course." Kat walked toward the door, but Flynn hadn't moved. Was he going to stop her? Could she stay? As Kat walked by him, she traced a fingertip down his arm. His head turned but she caught a glimpse of his eyes closed, jaw taut. He stood still, waiting for her to pass. It was mean to tease him for her own education. The door closed; she paced down the dark hallway.

When the door opened again, Flynn was dressed in his usual jeans and t-shirt. "It's safe to come in now. Find anything interesting while you snooped through my room?"

"No, not really. You're kind of boring," Kat smirked at him and he chuckled.

"If you're so bored, perhaps I should take you home."

"I think I can manage. Plus, I don't want to go home. Can I stay here forever?" Flynn's jaw tightened again, and he stepped closer to her. Afternoon light from his window illuminated her face. His hand came up to brush her wavy hair from her eyes; Kat blushed and looked away.

"Why do you do that?" he whispered.

"Do what?"

"Look away."

"Because being this close to people makes me uncomfortable."

"Because they hurt you?"

"Not everyone, but yes. I'm just not used to this."

"Oh come on, I bet you've had boyfriends."

"I've had friends that are boys, with a few potential interests. But usually they either want to get physical or get intimate."

"What's the difference?"

Kat laughed. "They wanted to get in my pants or get to know more about my personal life. We couldn't just talk about art or movies or the latest political race.

They wanted to pick me up from my house and meet my parents. They wanted me to become this needy girlfriend that they could rescue."

"And you don't want to be rescued?"

"I'll rescue myself when the time comes. I certainly don't need a man to save me."

"Gotcha." Flynn dropped his hand. Kat picked it up again and interlaced their fingers.

"But I want you." Their eyes met, and Kat almost gasped with the spark she felt in her belly. She couldn't look away, and as much as it scared her, she knew she never would. She may not need a man, and it was true, but she wanted this man to stand next to her forever. Would he? Did he even like her?

Flynn leaned forward to graze her lips with his. It was a soft, sweet kiss, gentle and quick. "I want you, too. You have no idea."

"You're right. I don't."

"Maybe I'll explain it one day. For now, let's go." Flynn pulled her by the hand, grabbing his leather jacket on the way out the door.

"Where are we going?"

"Into the light."

Glynn is amazing. And I want so badly to just give in to him, even though he's only here for another week or so. I was in such a dark place just a few weeks ago, and I still feel that dark force pulling me down. I may have more of a reason to stay above the surface of the water, but my ankles are still tethered to the bottom of the pool. I still straddle that fence. I'm still clinging to the edge of the cliff face, trying to pull myself out of the vast hole that began eating away at me years ago. He makes things easy for a while, but when he drives away, the shadows rise again.

Kat knocked on the front door to Hunter's house. It had been about a month since his death, and Kat felt compelled to talk to him. She thought being close to him, or his house, rather, would be the next best thing. Mrs. Richardson answered the door.

"Kat, so nice to see you. Welcome. Please come in."

His mother looked older, with deepened wrinkles and grayer hair. Her motherly smile was gone. Kat stepped over the threshold and noticed that the house felt different, too. Hunter wasn't in the house, and his home was colder somehow.

"I hope it's not too much trouble. I just wanted…"

"I know, dear." Mrs. Richardson still had her mother radar. Maybe that never went away. "Actually, it's good you came by. I have something for you. Let's go upstairs."

"Something for me?"

"Yes. Hunter's father and I have finally started going through his things, and I found his guitar. I thought you might want it."

Kat was glad that she was following Mrs. Richardson up the stairs so she couldn't see her reaction. Memories blinded Kat: hot summer days sitting on the porch listening as Hunter played his guitar and wrote songs. She even had a CD of his music from a songwriter's camp he'd attended one year.

"I would like that very much."

"Good, I'm glad. It's just in here in his closet."

Kat hesitated in the doorway to Hunter's bedroom. She should have known that this would be hard. Tears threatened. For a bittersweet moment, she didn't think to see Hunter lounging on his bed or sitting in his office chair. The room had been cleaned, the bed stripped. His movie posters still crowded the walls, and his trophies cluttered the top of his dresser. "As you can see, we are still working on it."

"I understand. I can't imagine it's easy."

Mrs. Richardson turned to Kat and looked as if she were going to explain, tell all of the gory details of what a mother feels to lose her only child, especially one so young. Instead, she clutched her hands to her heart, took a sweeping gaze around the room, and turned back to the closet door to retrieve the guitar case. "Here ya go, sweetheart."

"Are you sure you don't want to keep it?"

"Oh yes, we have plenty of memories and photos and other things."

"Thank you, Mrs. Richardson."

"Oh, please call me Dawn. You can stay in here for a while if you want. Just holler if you need anything; I'll be in the kitchen."

Kat stood in the middle of Hunter's room, holding the guitar case by the handle with her fingers, and absorbed it: There was still a hint of his smell, but it was covered with Lysol and carpet cleaner. His computer was on. His parents were probably going through his files. How awful. Kat almost choked up thinking about the silence of this house now. She had placed her photographs in a shoebox in her own closet. She didn't pull them out to look at them, but every time she passed the closet door, she saw them in her mind. That was a lot different from sitting in this room and going through his things, touching his prized possessions, learning his secrets. The room would no longer hear the comfort of his conversation or bring out his you'll-always-forgive-me smile.

Mrs. Richardson had dusted as well, probably the first time the room got such treatment in all of Hunter's teenage years. Kat knew he certainly hadn't done it. She had wanted to come here to be closer to him. Instead, the room reopened the hole in her heart. The reminder of him only made it clearer that he would never come back.

But he had lived. The photos taped to the walls told a great story; she knew because she was in a lot of them and had heard the tales. Kat even saw a few of her own photographs of the pier and ones she'd taken at school.

She inhaled and made the most difficult step: out of the room. Hunter had lived, and he had left his mark, but it wasn't in that room. It was inside of her. She didn't need to see his possessions to remember him. She just needed to remember herself, her own life.

Kat headed back to the kitchen to say goodbye to Mrs. Richardson and thank her again for the guitar.

"Oh please, come sit down," Mrs. Richardson said. "I have a fresh batch of cookies coming out of the oven any second. Want one?"

Kat couldn't think of anything she wanted more. "Sure, thank you. Again."

"You are welcome." Mrs. Richardson took the cookie sheet out of the oven and placed it on the counter on a cutting board. They smelled divine. "It's nice to have a young person in the house," she said softly. She placed two on a small white plate and set the plate on the table. "Sit. Eat."

Kat immediately sat down. Mrs. Richardson had used the mom voice. Now she sat across the little table from Kat with a plate of her own. They took big bites of the warm chocolate chip treat.

"These are really good," Kat said.

"Thank you, dear. I felt like a pick-me-up. So how are you these days? It's been so long since you were here."

Kat cleared her throat. She tried to block out the images of her last visit. "I've been good."

"Oh, come on. I haven't lost my touch. Talk to me." After a pause, Mrs. Richardson seemed to remember who Kat was and continued, "I'm sorry. You only have to talk if you want to."

"No, it's okay. It's a lot to explain, and I've been doing better these days. I guess I came here because I felt lost."

Mrs. Richardson continued to bite into her cookie, so Kat opened the vault.

"I feel like I'm just drifting through life—some days I'm up and some days I'm super down. It can change from hour to hour. I like to think I'm pretty strong and can deal with a lot, but I almost prefer to turn off my brain and roam around on autopilot. I know that's bad. Because I should feel. I am alive. I am young…" Kat glanced at Hunter's mother, with an apology on her tongue, but the wise woman shook her head and urged Kat to keep going.

"I should be figuring out what I want to do with the rest of my life, but I can't even figure out what I want to do with the rest of my week. Party with friends? Sure. Hang out with Flynn? God, yes. I'll even still do my homework and go to class, but in the back of my mind, I'm outside running down the middle of a dark street. I can't tell if I'm running toward something or away from it."

Mrs. Richardson finally reached out to stop her by touching her hand. "Sweetie, you are doing great."

"Pssh. Yeah."

"No, you listen to me now. It's very simple, Kat. All of life's decisions can be made with your head, your heart, or your gut. First, you listen to your head. If you still don't know, you listen to your heart. Sometimes, if you think that your heart is biased, you go with your gut. There are no wrong answers. There are only winding paths to life's grand journey. Your journey is your own."

Kat couldn't reply. The simple wisdom clogged her throat. A weight had lifted from Kat's heart with the words. Could it all really be so easy? Mrs. Richardson stood and pulled Kat up to gather her in a hug. It was a classic mother's hug, and Kat remembered them well from her own mother, when times had been easier. Kat burrowed her face in Mrs. Richardson's neck, wrapped her arms around the woman's shoulders, and sighed. There was no telling whether it would come back tomorrow, but in this moment, Kat needed this mother's unconditional affection as much as this mother needed a child to wrap in her embrace.

Kat untangled from the hug, and Mrs. Richardson placed a hand on either side of Kat's face. "You'll be fine, sweetie. Trust yourself."

Kat nodded and stepped away. She leaned down and grabbed for the guitar case. "Well, I should probably go." She turned once more to say something, anything, to thank this woman for healing her just a little bit. She opened her mouth and gestured with a hand, as if to catch the words in the air, but nothing came out.

Mrs. Richardson nodded. "I know. It was so good to see you. Please visit again soon. And I hope you find good use for that guitar. I know Hunter would be glad that you have it."

They walked in silence to the front door as Kat composed herself.

"Thank you. I will. Goodbye."

# CHAPTER TWELVE

*Bailey*

On Tuesday morning, Bailey embarked on the seven-hour drive back to school. He thought back on his visit home. His father hadn't spoken to him or his mother all of Monday. He cooked spaghetti for the family for his last dinner home, and his father sat with them in silence. At 2 a.m., Katie strolled in and found Bailey asleep in front of the television. She had reeked of smoke and alcohol but not on her breath; her friends were at it again.

Bailey was glad that he had visited. His mother truly appreciated his help around the house and with Kat, too. She had looked into his eyes that night on her bed and had seen the man he was trying so desperately to become. If she saw it, then it had to be in there somewhere. The test would be to see if that man was inside of him without the constant reminder of his father for motivation.

He called Lina. "What's up, baby girl?"

"Hey, Bailey. I'm not doing much. What about you?"

"Driving back."

"How'd it go?"

"Alright. How are you? I'd love to talk about anything but my family right now."

"Okay, let's see. The Boob is calling me now. He wants to see me."

"Don't do it, Lin."

"I know, but he's so sweet. He's really sorry. He says we can take it slow."

"Don't do it. You are so much better than that scum."

"Where are all of these guys then, Bailey? Where are the ones that you approve of?"

"No man is good enough for you."

"Great. So I live my life alone? With only you?"

"Hey. I'm not saying that you'll end up alone, but no man will ever be able to treat you well enough. It's because of the nature of men."

"I want to get married. I want to have babies."

"Whoa."

"Not now, dumbass. I just thought that by now I'd be in a relationship that was leaning toward those goals. Instead, I have to wait for a beginning again."

"Why don't we get married?"

"Be serious."

"No, I am. Like when we're older."

"Like when we're thirty?"

"Maybe fifty."

"Ha. Just so you can keep your options open for as long as possible."

"Pretty much." Bailey grinned at Lina's soft chuckle.

"Fifty is too old to have babies."

"Yeah, can't help you there."

"Oh, I see."

"Hey, I said the nature of men, and I am a man. I'm not perfect either, Lina."

"You're close. Anyway, I'm going to London this summer. I'm so excited!"

"When?"

"The first three weeks in June. We're going to Soho, Theatreland."

"What's that?"

"Exactly what the name says. It's where all of the famous London plays are put on, streets upon streets of theater."

"That actually sounds really cool."

"You're telling me. I just have to survive hell month at school and then another semester."

"You can do it."

"I know I can. I just want to be sane at the end of it all."

"Well, are you sure you're sane now?"

"Hey now, don't joke."

"You're fine. Every college student feels hopeless about two and a half months in when finals and projects are piling up."

"Speaking of…"

"No. You have to keep me company. I have four more hours to go."

"Bailey, I have three papers due next week."

"Okay, tell me about them. I have nothing else to do."

"Well, my first one is pretty interesting. It's on Wikipedia and the undependability of its acclaimed unbiased source of information."

"You could pop out a thesis on that in your sleep. Next!"

"Okay, the second one is slightly more difficult. I have to write five to seven pages on the playwright Suzan-Lori Parks. My topic is repetition and how she uses it to support her main textual points."

"Um...I have no idea what you said after playwright. But I know you can do it!"

"My third is a technical essay on digital printing within publishing houses."

"Wow, that sounds like loads of fun. Alright, I'll let you go. Write well, and call me back if you get bored. I will be."

"Okay, Bailey. Drive safe. Talk to you later, bud."

"Bye."

Bailey popped in the soundtrack to *The Last Samurai* and passed the next four hours listening mindlessly.

He willed time to move faster. When he saw signs for Charleston, his foot pressed harder on the accelerator. He switched to the radio and sang loudly to random songs. Knowing home was just another half hour away pepped him up a bit.

To celebrate being back in the wonderful big C, Bailey headed straight to Bill's pub. He thought of Jasmine and smelled her hair in a sudden gush of wind. He missed her. He left his overnight bag in the car along with other "necessities" from his mother packed. At the pub, he welcomed the smell of beer and cigarettes, even though he didn't smoke.

Jasmine came out from the back with a full tray of shot glasses as he entered the main bar. Bailey pondered taking one from her and angering a customer. He didn't want to bring aggravation to her shift, however.

"Hey, Jaz."

She spun with expertise, not spilling a drop.

"Hey, stranger. Give me a second. There's a table of men playing hooky in the back corner."

"Okay. I'll change it up and sit by the window."

Bailey wanted to take Jasmine out. He wanted to do something special for her. He felt a newfound confidence that life could be better if you made it that way, and he wanted to make a real effort. Where would he take her? What would they do?

"Here you go, babe." Jasmine set a Coke beside a napkin he'd torn up.

"Thanks," he said. He'd take her cosmic bowling. She and Jack used to do that all the time; she'd beat his friend and gloat. Jack was a sore loser. Bailey realized he could look back on those days with more calm resolve than frustration. Yet the image of Jasmine's battered face, like his mother's, would never leave him.

———◦———

*"Oh, don't be such a sore loser."*

*"You cheated."*

*"How do you cheat at bowling? A computer tallies how many pins you knock down."*

*"I don't know."*

*"Just admit it. I kicked your ass."*

*"Whatever."*

*"Party pooper!"*

*"What's going on?" Bailey asked as Jasmine and Jack entered his apartment.*

"We went bowling. I beat him by a lot, and he's pouting."

"Oh, come on Jack! Jasmine is no ordinary woman. Just pretend she's one of the guys. Will that lessen the blow?"

"No. Because I fuck her, Bail. Thinking of her as a dude will screw with my brain."

"Alright, then. What's up his butt?" Bailey directed the question to Jasmine.

"I'm not sure. But he's actually been like this since before we went out."

"Jack! Why are you pouting over bowling? Jack?" Bailey followed Jack to see why his friend wasn't joining in the fun. In Bailey's bedroom, Jack was looking at a photo on the nightstand of Bailey and Zoe. "Dude?"

"Mind your own damn business, Bailey."

"I'm your friend and curious, is all."

"I said back off."

"Fine, okay, just tell me everything is okay with you." Bailey didn't see Jack put down the picture, but in a flash Jack had shoved him back hard, slamming him into the bedroom door.

"Bailey!" Jasmine rushed around the corner. Bailey still leaned against the door. Jack was steaming with tension. She *glared at each man with disappointment and confusion. She slowly backed away, grabbed her bag from the couch, and walked out the door. When the door closed behind her, Jack snapped to and ran after her.*

*Bailey grabbed some Tylenol from the bathroom. The pair of them had come and gone so quickly, he didn't even recognize the shift from Jasmine's enthusiasm to Jack's anger. The mood swings were starting to get to him.*

---

"Jasmine, I think we should go out," Bailey said as he walked Jasmine home; it was just about dinnertime.

"What? You told me just weeks ago we shouldn't."

"I know I said that. But I want to take you out somewhere for some fun. Being home shifted my outlook a little."

"Where? When?"

"I'm not sure. I was thinking some dinner at Sticky Fingers followed by some cosmic bowling?"

"Not tonight or tomorrow. I have a huge paper due Thursday on Monet."

"Just let me know when you need a night off. I have that Martin Luther research paper due in about a week."

"Get on it then!"

"Yeah, yeah."

They had arrived at her apartment stoop. Standing at the base of the stairs, Bailey wanted to touch her. He wanted to kiss her. There was a significant difference between talking about going out for fun and crossing into a physical relationship. Jasmine reached into her bag for her keys. She held them in her hand, jingling them among her fingers.

"Do you want to come up?"

"Yes, I do."

"Are you going to come up?"

"Do you want me to?"

Jasmine looked down at her feet, took a step forward so their torsos brushed, and lifted her head to look him in the face. He hated when she did that. All he could see, smell, taste, was her.

"Yes. I'll make you a peanut butter and jelly sandwich for dinner."

"How can I resist that?"

"You can't. Come on. It's about to rain."

He'd never been in her apartment. The place was beautiful: hardwood floors, painted walls, sheer curtains, lots of space because she didn't have much furniture, and a magnificent bay window overlooking the street.

"How did you find this place?"

"I know the contractor who redid this place. When he came in to do renovations, I happened to mention that I was lined up to move in. I posed a few questions to him."

"You're clever, and it paid off."

"Don't you underestimate me."

"I won't ever again."

"How about that PB and J?"

Bailey grimaced a bit. He asked, "Don't you have anything else in this amazing apartment?"

"Artwork?" She smiled at him, poking fun.

"I'm going to have to start buying you groceries. It pains me to know you get that great figure from PB and J and eggs, which I make, mind you."

"I eat stuff sometimes. Most of it is what I can grab for free at the pub."

"I was afraid of that."

"There's my refrigerator. Take a look. I'll be right back." Jasmine passed through a side door. She didn't close the door all the way, so Bailey watched her set her bag next to a computer desk and unzip her hooded sweatshirt. Underneath, she wore a clingy tank top that stopped inches above baggy painter's pants. Bailey swallowed hard. Maybe he should skip food and just go home?

"Hey, Jaz?"

"Yeah," she said, exiting her room. Her feet were bare; he could see the dark blue polish on her toenails. Why were her toes so sexy?

"I think maybe I should go."

"Why? What happened?" She reached out to touch his arm.

"Nothing. I just feel like I shouldn't be up here. I guess now my brain is kicking in."

"That's no good."

"Actually it's very good, for you especially."

"Bailey, why are you so nervous?"

"I'm at one of those moments when I feel like I'm about to lose control and do something I'll regret."

"You want to hit me?"

"No, no. I…fuck it."

Bailey crossed to her, slid a hand on either side of her face, and kissed her. Her body tensed with surprise, but then she relaxed and let her hands grip his shoulders. For years, he had imagined how it would feel to touch these lips.

"I'm sorry," he muttered, placing his forehead to hers. "That's what I was afraid would happen. I saw you take off your sweater, and I couldn't think."

"You don't have to be afraid. We deserve this, Bailey."

"God, I hope you're right. I care about you, Jaz. I don't want to rush anything."

"I don't either. I want this time to be special."

"Show me your paintings."

"What?"

"Will you?"

"Sure. I guess. That's kind of random."

"I desperately need a distraction. Ever since your show last year, I've remembered that your paintings evoke emotions and strength. I haven't seen your new stuff."

"Come with me." Jasmine led him down the opposite end of her apartment hallway to a closed door. "This is my studio."

"Oh, I thought it was the living room since your easel is in there."

"Yes, I have a setup there, but I'm serious in here. Sometimes I go in and surround myself with my work. It fills me up. They are so personal; I'm not even sure I want to show you. Now I'm scared."

"Don't be."

"Okay. Here goes nothing." She opened the door and sucked in a big breath. She let it out again when he turned back to her with a big smile on his face. One easel held a Monet reproduction in progress.

"That's to go along with my paper."

Bailey stood in the middle of the room and spun in slow circles. Jasmine was talented. There was such diversity in her work: landscapes in watercolor, profiles in oils, architecture in black ink. Swirls of color were everywhere.

"You're amazing." She chuckled sheepishly. "No, I'm serious. Your work is so vibrant, just like I thought it would be. I had no idea, though, that you'd capture so many different...is the word genres?"

"Sure, you can think of it that way."

"How should I think about it?"

"They're called mediums actually. But I just paint or draw what I feel is right at the moment."

"I love this one," he said, indicating a sketch drawing of a woman sitting on a bench. Despite the indefinite lines from her pencil, he could still see the age in the subject's face.

"I drove down to Savannah for a weekend. She was just sitting there practically inviting me to capture her."

"It really is amazing, Jaz. I only wish I could capture something, either like you with images or with words. Lina, and my mom for that matter, can sit one rainy afternoon and write pages and pages of insightful stuff. I just have a knack for historical dates and religious philosophies."

"Bailey, everyone is different. I can't write or memorize dates, but I have this." She pointed around the room. "I don't know what I'd do if I couldn't release some energy with my artwork. I work hard at the pub so I can buy supplies. Art stores know their shit; they charge you a lot of money for cheap brushes and paint brands. So, I have to pay a lot more to get the good stuff."

"Are you going to have any other shows soon?"

"No. I'm focusing on building my portfolio. When I host a show, I'll have an array of pieces to choose from.

Last time, I had to put everything I'd done into the show just to fill the space they allotted me."

"So what do you do now to get your name out there and stuff?"

"I'm going back to the studio I worked at last summer. I paint and work on other creative pieces with a local artist in North Carolina. We bond over messiness, and he spouts my name around at dinner parties."

"A man, eh?"

"He's my grandfather. Jealous?"

"No."

"Well, what do you say to a quickie dinner? I don't know about you, but I have to finish that paper and the painting on the easel. I hate how professors assume that creativity constantly flows through my veins."

"I know what you mean. I can always tell whether a paper will come back with a good grade or not; it all depends on whether I'm in the zone when I'm writing it."

"Auto Zone?"

"Shut up."

"Sorry." Jasmine pulled ingredients from the cabinet and the refrigerator: a loaf of bread, a jar of peanut butter, and a jar of jelly. Because there was so little furniture, they sat on the bay windowsill, facing each other.

"This really is a nice place."

"I know. I'm going to hate having to move."

"Move?"

"I can't stay here forever. Plus, when I go to North Carolina for the summer, I'll either have to sublet it or move out early."

"What would happen if you just stayed and apprenticed under a local artist here?"

"I don't know anyone here."

"Even with that show last year?"

"My Pepe would be so sad if I didn't return to North Carolina to work with him." Jasmine smiled with a mouthful of peanut butter. She was still sexy.

"I'm sure. Thank you for the wonderful sandwich. But I should probably be on my way now so you can work."

"And you should work, too, mister."

They both got up from the windowsill, leaving their plates. For a moment, they stood facing one another, silent yet unwilling to move. Jasmine finally turned toward the door. She stood on her tiptoes and kissed him. The kiss was quick, but it was still a shock to his system. He waved, unsure of what to say, and she shut the door. Heading down the stairs, he heard loud music come from her apartment: classical piano. Jasmine was certainly intriguing, with different facets that all seemed to fit her just right.

# CHAPTER THIRTEEN

*Kat*

A text message alert made Kat roll over in bed. It was too early. She groped for her phone on the nightstand, her eyes still stubbornly closed. One eye popped open to glare at the screen. A smile spread across her face when she saw the text was from Flynn. Next Saturday he had to leave for his job, and they had been spending a lot of time together.

His text read: "Wake up and come outside."

She replied: "But I'm still sleeping."

Within seconds, another message appeared: "You have 20 min to get your cute ass out here."

Kat lay in her comfortable, warm bed and seriously considered blowing him off. She wanted to roll over and sleep for another couple of hours. The sun barely showed behind the curtains. But her smile spread again, thinking of Flynn waiting for her. Kat threw the comforter aside and ran to the bathroom to speed through a shower.

When she was clean and moderately presentable, Kat ran back into her bedroom wrapped in an oversized towel. What to wear? Where were they going? She ditched her normal uniform of jeans and a t-shirt for a black tank top and jean skirt. She'd show off some leg today before it got too cold outside. She dug in the back of her closet for the red leather jacket she had inherited from her grandmother. She had never worn it, and for a moment, she sniffed the collar to soak in the familiar perfume. A pair of black flip-flops sealed the deal.

Kat snuck down the hallway, noticing the clock said it was just past seven. She tiptoed past her parents' bedroom and heard familiar snores. Just to be safe, she pulled her cell from her pocket and texted her mother, whose phone was off for the night. She would receive the text when she woke: "Mom, went out with girlfriends, planning surprise birthday party, be back later." Maybe it wasn't a lie because she didn't actually know what she was doing today.

Kat snuck out the front door and let out a sigh of relief that she had made it out without waking anyone. Flynn leaned against his car with a sexy smirk on his face. God, she could eat him up. "Wow, babe. You have legs. Nice legs, at that."

"Shut up," Kat giggled. She sauntered down the stoop steps, exaggerating her leg movements. "You know you like it."

As Kat approached, Flynn reached for her hips to pull her in for a kiss. With his face hovering close to hers, he said, "Yes, I do. You look beautiful. You seem to have a glow. Oh my God, are you pregnant?" He pushed her back to scrutinize her face.

Kat punched him in the chest. "No, doofus. You have to have sex to get pregnant."

"You do?" He feigned confusion. "Wow. That explains a lot."

"You're weird. Where are we going?"

"I thought you might want to come with me when I go out to Virginia Beach to check out the new apartment. Meet my friends, check out the area." Flynn smiled down at her.

"Sure, that sounds like fun. How far is it?"

"About an hour?"

"Okay, let's go."

In the car, Flynn plugged his iPod into the sound system, and they spent the hour poking fun at each other's musical tastes and concert band wish lists. During lulls in their conversation, Flynn reached over and touched Kat's thigh. She relished the feel of her newly exposed, smooth skin. She felt sexy. Not stressed or worried or anxious; she felt happy.

Shortly after, Flynn pulled into an apartment complex near the beach. She could smell the salt in the air as she got out of the car. Flynn pulled out his cell to make a call, and she heard him say, "Hey buddy, I'm here."

Soon, a guy in black boxers with red hearts and a rumpled white t-shirt appeared in slippers at a nearby door.

"Dude, nice outfit," Flynn said as the guy walked toward them.

"Bite me, Flynn. Why are you here this early? I pulled the nightshift last night and only got a couple hours of sleep."

"Well, why didn't you send Charlie down?"

"He's over at Ronnie's, probably sleeping too."

"I'm sorry. We wanted to spend the day looking around. Luke, this is Kat." Flynn turned to her and reached for her hand. "Kat, this is Luke, an old friend. Luke and Charlie will be my roommates. Alright, dude, let's check out what you guys found."

Luke gave Kat a once-over and said, "'Sup."

Kat waved back, feeling strangely shy around this sleep-deprived stranger. She was just getting to know Flynn, and now she realized he had a whole life of stories and friends that she knew nothing about.

As the three headed into the apartment, Luke said, "It's great, man." He opened the door and ushered them all in. "A bedroom for each of us, large living room, as you can see, and decent kitchen. Two full baths. And the best part…" Luke strolled through the living room to the sliding glass door. "A balcony overlooking the ocean."

The sea breeze and damp air whipped across their faces as they stepped out onto the balcony. It was large enough for a small, round grill and two folding chairs. Kat finally spoke, "Wow."

Flynn squeezed her hand. "I know, right? You guys chose well. I can't imagine we can afford this place, though."

"We're cops. We get a discount. Plus, no one wants to be on the first floor. We'll make it work. And although Charlie's name is on the lease, I'm not sure how much of him we're going to see."

"He's still hot with Ronnie?"

"Yeah."

"Why doesn't he just move in with her?"

"Won't commit. He likes having an exit strategy," Luke said, glancing over at Kat. "Sorry."

She replied, "Don't worry about it."

"One less guy stinking up the bathroom," Flynn said.

Luke chuckled, "Right?"

They stepped back into the kitchen. "Feel free to look around. I'm gonna go reunite with my pillow. Oh yeah, dark curtains. Buy them. They will save your life." With that, Luke vanished down the hall to the left, and they heard a door shut. Kat and Flynn looked at each other and laughed.

"He seems nice."

"Yeah, he's a good guy."

"How do you know him?"

"We went to high school together and decided to go through the academy. Come on, let's see if we can find my room." Flynn pulled her down the hall where Luke had disappeared. One door at the end of the hall stood open. It was the only source of light down the long hallway.

The room was empty. With sunlight pouring in through a large window, the beige carpet and white walls almost blinded them after walking down the dark hallway. "I brought some stuff. It's in the trunk of my car. I'll go grab it. Stay here and plan where my shit is gonna go."

"Need any help?"

"Nah, I got it. I'll be right back." Flynn gave her a quick kiss on the temple before leaving the room.

Kat circled the empty room to assess the potential. She knew nothing of feng shui, but her artist's eye could usually shift over to a decent interior decorator's instinct.

After a few minutes, Flynn returned carrying two boxes. He set them on the floor and looked around for Kat.

"Psst." She hissed from the floor.

"What the hell?"

"I think your bed should go right here."

Flynn laughed. "Oh yeah? That's the spot?"

"Yeah, come over here and see for yourself."

"Yes, ma'am." Flynn crouched down to lie beside her. The closet was not too far to his right, the large window on the wall to the left. Honestly, there weren't many options. His dresser would fit on the wall opposite. He probably would have to leave his office desk behind.

"What do you think?"

"I like it. You chose well."

"Thank you, sir."

"This bed is kind of uncomfortable, though. Not a lot of cushion," Flynn said. Kat rolled to one side to be closer to him. She rested her head on his shoulder and her hand at his heart. "Oh wait, I think it's improving a bit."

"I could fall asleep for sure."

"No, no. We have a lot to do today."

"Nooo," she mumbled into his shirt. "Sleep. Someone woke me up really early today."

"We have to go to the store. I want to pick up my share of rations: toilet paper, cleaning supplies, you know. And then I'd like to stop by my precinct office to see my captain."

"Okay, fine. If I can't entice you."

"Well, we do have all day." Flynn reached for the hand on his chest, brought it up to his lips, and kissed her palm. "But I don't think you're ready, Kat."

She closed her eyes to hide the truth from him. He was right. While she was drawn to him, attracted to him, she still held back a part of herself because, if she was being honest, she didn't fully trust him. It wasn't because of anything he had or hadn't done. They really hadn't known each other long, and letting people in was a challenge for her.

Flynn lifted her chin so that she had no choice but to look into his eyes. "I can feel your walls coming down. But there is still a shield up. I get it, Kat, really I do. You are protecting yourself, and I get that it's ingrained in you. I just want you to feel safe around me."

"I do. I just can't explain it."

"You don't like being vulnerable. Mostly because every time you've let yourself be open to other people, they hurt you. All I can do is try every day to prove to you that I won't. And Kat, we are all afraid of being hurt. Maybe you'll end up breaking my heart." He smiled at her to lighten the mood. "Maybe you'll fall in love with Luke. Those were some hot boxer shorts."

Kat appreciated that he was being honest with her but also trying to keep the day light. He always seemed to understand what she needed, whether she did or not. She wanted to show him that she cared for him, a lot, but her fear could be paralyzing.

"You have a point. And with that sleepy, baritone voice of his. I might not be able to control myself."

"Note to self: buy ugly boxer shorts." Flynn kissed her lightly on the lips. She could sense that he wanted to be gentle with her. She caressed his cheek, which made her fingers itch from the whiskers on his chin. Relishing the unrushed pressure from his mouth, she relaxed her body into his. Flynn's hand slid around her waist, down her back, and cupped her butt. Kat thought of smiling, remembering his cute ass comment. Then his hand drifted lower to the hemline of her skirt. He traced the back of her knee and brought her leg up around his hip. He rolled backwards, taking her with him, so her body was flush on top of him.

Her hair fell around both of their faces, enveloping them in a curtain of rich chocolate brown. Kat broke the kiss but didn't move. She couldn't move because Flynn's hands held her hips in place, to keep her balanced. "You don't need new boxer shorts. As long as you're not rocking tighty-whities under those jeans, our future looks bright."

She vibrated from his laughter. Kat sat up, leaving her straddling Flynn's waist. His hands remained on her hips. He said, "Don't move."

"What? What's wrong? Is someone here?" Kat peered around, suspicious and tense.

"No. I just don't want you to move. It would make things…harder for me." Kat blushed as the meaning of his words became clear. She moved off of his lap and made herself stand. Flynn groaned. "Alright, let's go."

"Probably for the best."

"If you say so." Flynn stood as well, and he reached for her hand once again.

Backstage during the play last year, I was helping out with set design. There was this techie boy, one of those guys who checked microphones and lights. We were hanging out in one of the dressing rooms behind the stage one late afternoon during a dress rehearsal. Everyone else was on stage or at their stations, but we weren't needed just then. We sat on a cracked leather sofa and made out like we were in a kissing contest. It was rushed and awkward, and I felt very little. More than anything else, I was more excited I was having my first kiss. He seemed happy to have a green light. With Flynn, the kisses matter more. He is a great kisser, but I am nervous about him. I want to be better for him.

Flynn and Kat spent the day driving around Virginia Beach, buying supplies for Flynn's move next week. They decided to walk downtown and check out the local shops, get familiar with the community. All of the main street shops were common: a barber, an antiques shop, and lots of cafes. When they came upon a used bookstore, Kat clutched Flynn's hand. "Can we go in? I love used bookstores."

"Absolutely. I aim to please." Flynn opened the shop door for her and ushered her in before him. Kat stopped in her tracks. There was barely enough room to walk around with all of the floor-to-ceiling bookshelves. Each shelf was stuffed with paperbacks crammed sideways and stacked every which way. The brilliance of it made Kat's head hurt because where would she begin? It would take days, months even, to go shelf by shelf and book by book. She should narrow it down by genre.

"What's wrong? Man, what is that smell?"

"Knowledge. Or rather, it's glue and aging pages. I love that smell."

"Wow, you really dig this, don't you?"

"Yes." Kat gazed in awe at the expanse of the shelves. She wondered if there was another floor or perhaps several back rooms outside of her line of sight.

"Then why are we standing in the entrance?"

"I'm trying to figure out where to look first."

"Well, what kind of book are you looking for?"

"I don't need a specific book. I just like to roam the aisles, reading random titles and seeing what I have to take home. A person's library says a lot about them. Kind of like the things I learned about you through your iPod music library. Only different," Kat explained. She had decided to explore the main aisle and read the genre labels at the end of each row. New Releases. General Fiction. Chick Lit. Mystery. Sci-Fi. Romance. Nonfiction.

Kat doubled back to Mystery and darted down the aisle. She trailed her index finger down the nearest row of books then stopped midway to start her one-on-one search. Flynn stood back and watched her. She forgot he existed and became engrossed in the books around her.

Kat was reading the back of a thick paperback when Flynn asked, "What did you find?"

"Oh, just a book."

"Yes, I can see that. What's it about?"

"It's a suspense thriller about a serial rapist that roams college campuses and victimizes young women. It sounds really good."

"Oh yeah. Who wouldn't be excited about rape?"

Kat laughed. "You know what I mean."

"So do you want to be a writer?"

"I am a writer."

"I know. I mean when you go to school. What do you want to do for a living?"

"The infamous question. I wish I knew." Kat put the book back on the shelf. "I imagine that college will help me decide. Do I like writing? Of course. But I like reading, and I like art. I think, maybe, I could be a teacher because I love books. The possibilities are vast."

"Where do you want to go to school?"

"That's a harder question. I've just started doing the research on different schools and different programs. Why did you choose not to go to college?"

"Um, I was never good at school. I mean I went through the motions, but I never cared the way teachers thought I should. In my mind, I wanted to be out in the world doing things. So I decided to try the police academy."

"And your parents were supportive?"

"Not at first. They thought it was just a way for me to get out of going to college and advancing myself. But when they saw I was dedicated to the program, they came around."

"What about Mel?"

"Art school in New York."

"But how is she going to market that? I mean make a profitable profession from an art degree?"

"I don't know. I don't think she knows. But sometimes, Kat, it's not always about money. She'll figure it out. Or she won't. But it's my parents' dime, not mine."

"Good for her."

"What does that mean?"

"It's just good that she is following her passion. That she knows with such clarity what it is that drives her."

"What drives you, Kat?"

She scanned the shelves of books to buy herself some time to think. Wasn't she trying to answer that question? For so long, she had listened to what her parents thought she should be doing with her life. It was their voices she heard even now, not her own. Her answer was simple, "I want to be free."

"What?"

"When I think of my future, I see one blurry image where I'm wearing a business skirt-suit and high heels.

I'm in a high-rise building in a city, in a corner office because there are windows everywhere. And I'm sitting at a huge reddish-brown glazed desk. I have the impression that it's a publishing house. Maybe that's why I'm drawn to books. Despite what I'm wearing or where I am, it's the freedom of the cityscape and the inherent success and financial independence that stir me. I want to stand on my own two feet and know that my accomplishments are mine. In my dream, I am respected and sought out for them."

"That's a worthy dream."

"But is it just a dream? You know, my dad says: 'You'll never get anywhere unless you know where you're going.'"

"That's deep. But sometimes you just have to go with the flow. Like today. Today was a lot of fun, just being with you, walking around, taking care of business without the pressure of timelines."

Kat smiled up at him. "Yeah, it was fun. Does that mean we have to go back now?"

"Soon. I just have to do one more thing."

"What's that?"

"Buy you that serial rapist book." Flynn grabbed for the book and sprinted to the cash register.

"What? Wait, no…" Kat ran after him, laughing down the aisle.

> Can it really be that simple? To go to school for what you love? Find your passion and follow it? I feel like I have two lives ahead of me: the one where I choose what comes next and I'm happy, but I might be poor. And the other where I have financial security, but I feel the same loneliness that follows me now. How do I choose? I know enough not to dream for both.

"So, will I see you again?"

Kat and Flynn leaned against the hood of his car in her driveway. The setting sun filtered through Kat's wavy hair, giving it a reddish hue.

"I hope so. I still have a lot to do before I move."

"I see." Kat tried to ignore the heaviness weighing on her heart.

"Hey, listen to me." Flynn enveloped her face in his hands. Kat lifted her gaze to meet his. "I'm not moving to the moon. We can see each other still. I want to see you as much as I can. It's probably too early for this, but the day I met you changed my life."

"You don't have to do this."

"I'm not doing anything but telling you the truth. I am coming to know you. I get that you are trying something with me, but it scares you because you think I'm leaving you. I'm not leaving you. I wish I could whisk you away with me when I go. But you have to stay, and I have to go."

"I know." Kat reached up to remove Flynn's hands and hugged him.

"We'll talk. And we will visit."

"You'll be busy doing risky cop things."

"You really should stop reading mysteries."

"Never."

"Stubborn woman."

"You like it."

"I do."

Kat felt him pull away. "You should go inside. I'm sure your parents are spying on us from the window."

"I doubt it. I'll talk to you later. Good luck with the move."

"Thanks. I'll call you later." To seal their goodbye, he kissed her lightly on the lips. As he got in his car, Kat clenched her jaw to hold back the tears. Please don't let this be the last time she felt the warm pressure of those lips or the closeness of his heartbeat. Kat had been strong before Flynn came into her life, and she would manage after he left. At the end of the day, the only person she could really depend on was herself.

# CHAPTER FOURTEEN

## *Bailey*

B ailey tucked a plaid blanket under his arm. He was holding a picnic basket when he knocked on Jasmine's door. He'd run into one of her friends yesterday and made sure she would be out of class for the afternoon. She answered the door with a paintbrush in her mouth and wearing paint-splotched overalls, her hair up in a disorderly knot.

"I got an extension. I did the paper; the painting, though, I can't seem to finish."

"Then come on this wonderfully planned picnic. Even better, bring your painting and work outside. It's a gorgeous day. And you're gorgeous with that blue paint on your nose."

Jasmine rubbed the paint off. She hesitated before answering, "I suppose."

"Oh, come on. What better way to get inspired to do a landscape than to be outside?"

"Okay. Let me get my stuff together. Come in for a minute. That basket looks heavy; what's in it?"

"Champagne for an appetizer. Cashew-crusted chicken breast for the main course, and strawberries and chocolate for dessert."

"Oh my God, Bailey."

"What? I wanted to do something special for you."

"This is special all right. I'll be right back."

Bailey set the basket on the counter, the blanket on top, and put his hands in his pockets while he waited. Jasmine came out of her studio with her messenger bag full of brushes and paints. The painting dangled from her right hand.

"Ready?"

"I think so." She glanced around her apartment. "Let's just go before I miss the best time of day."

"Okay. Here we go."

They walked a few blocks down from her apartment to a park near the waterfront. They found a nice patch of grass where Bailey opened the blanket.

"Is this good?"

"Yeah, it'll do. Should I wait to paint until after we eat?"

"Yes. I don't know how much longer the chicken will hold."

"Alright, then I'll have some of that champagne."

"Yes, ma'am."

Bailey popped the cork on the bottle and poured them each a small glass. They sat side by side in silence for a while, sipping the bubbly and enjoying the light breeze. Every few moments, Jasmine glanced at her painting to make sure grass hadn't blown on it or a dog hadn't relieved himself near her chosen spot.

"You were right. This is a nice day."

"Ready for food?"

"Yes."

Bailey pulled a Tupperware container from the basket with two pieces of chicken breast. Then he pulled out two plates, knives, and forks.

"They should still be warm according to the manual on my crazy temperature-securing container here."

"It will be fine." Jasmine cut a small piece and brought it to her mouth. Bailey watched as she tasted and chewed. "Mmmmm."

"Good. Okay." With her approval, Bailey felt secure enough to eat. Suddenly, Jasmine set down her plate of half-eaten chicken, scooted over to her bag, grabbed several tubes of paint and a clean palette, and began to mix colors. "Are you okay?"

"Yeah. I just got this great idea for a color to add to the sky. I tried to forget it and move on, but you can't move on when you don't get something right."

"I can understand that."

"It occurred to me that, if I mix these two colors, then the color combination should make the hues perfect."

"Well then, don't let the chicken get in your way."

"Oh, sorry. I'll eat in a second. I want to make sure this will work, mixing the colors."

"Won't the paint dry out if you let it sit for too long?"

"Do you remember when I said that I buy the expensive stuff?"

"Yes."

"I pay for my paint to *not* dry out. Wait for it…yes! Okay, back to wonderful food that was made for me by a handsome man." As she crawled back to her plate, she leaned toward him and kissed him. "You're cute."

"No," Bailey said. "Not with the cute."

"Sorry. But it's true. Thank you for this."

"You're very welcome."

Jasmine finished her chicken and lay back on the blanket to gaze at the sky. She sighed and rolled over to her canvas. She found a small, thin stick and pushed it into the ground at an angle to support the painting vertically. After she was satisfied, Jasmine removed every single tube of paint and brush from her bag and laid them out beside her on the blanket. Bailey watched, fascinated.

He relaxed, lying on his side and supporting his head with his hand. He even slipped off his shoes. Jasmine stared at her paints for a long time and then set into motion what Bailey imagined was a step-by-step procedure in her mind. She took the mixed paint on the palette and tested it in the top left corner of the canvas. Bailey smiled as she stuck out her tongue to focus on her task. How did she not go cross-eyed being that close to such a large canvas? When she seemed satisfied with the color mixture, Jasmine applied it periodically throughout her sky.

Bailey took advantage of the fine day and the actual sky to contemplate. How far away he seemed now from that broken boy in his childhood. He felt nothing but peace. He said to Jasmine, "You look so content with yourself."

"Are you kidding me? I am going crazy!"

"You don't look it. You are just staring and painting and staring some more."

"Well, inside my brain, it's more like: What color did I want to do that? What color should I do it? How will that impact the larger scheme? What was the assignment again?"

"Geez, I didn't know painting was so involved. I just thought you felt what to do and did it."

"Sure, I feel what to do. Intuition has a lot of influence over my overall decisions. That doesn't mean there aren't other voices in my head trying to distract me from the right path."

"I was thinking about paths just now, too."

"Oh yeah? Do tell. Don't worry, *you* won't distract me."

"I was just pondering life after college."

"No. Don't go there. I refuse to embrace that phase of my life."

"Okay. Are you going to stay enrolled at C of C forever?"

"No. But I can still live in my wonderful apartment in ignorance and bliss."

"Fair enough."

"I just have so much going on in the now that I can't think past my final projects for this semester."

"I don't think about my final projects. I complete them on a need-to-do basis."

"Ha. I can't conjure up a good piece of artwork just because the deadline is approaching with speed. This one I started three weeks ago, but I've actually had a recent drought in desire and motivation."

"It would be easier to bullshit a paper than a painting."

"Yes. Although there is some technique behind randomly picking colors and putting them in random places in whatever shapes come to mind. I believe it's called abstract art. For this assignment, though, when I'm supposed to be replicating the masterpieces of one of the best Impressionist painters of all time, there is significantly more pressure. Every color, every stroke, and every decision matters."

"Do you not have any freedom in the assignment?"

"Sure, but each independent gesture must be justified."

"Well, what you have already looks amazing. You can do it."

"Thanks, Bailey."

"So how many more of these things do you have to do before Christmas break?"

"I have two more for the same class to complete my portfolio. Luckily, though, I saved the most free-range pieces for last. They won't take as long to do."

"Cool. What are you going to paint?"

"One is a painting, and one is a drawing. I'm pondering the idea of doing a portrait. Can I draw you?"

The question took Bailey by surprise. He wasn't altogether sure how to respond.

"I don't know."

"You have such amazing features: big blue eyes, strong cheekbones, dark wavy hair."

"When would you want to do this? How long will it take?"

"Once I finish this, I need to get started. It could take a few sessions. We'll start with one afternoon, and I'll draw until you can't sit anymore."

"Alright. How about this weekend?"

"Friday night?"

"Some of my dorm mates have plans Friday night." She glanced over just as he smirked to himself, thinking of the debauchery and drinking, lots of drinking. "How about Saturday? I'll come over when I wake up."

"Okay. Don't be afraid, Bail."

"I'm not afraid. I just haven't ever had anyone draw me before."

"It'll be fun. And then if you like what I do, I can make a print copy for you."

"How do you do that?"

"I turn my picture into a slide that is sent off and comes back as a stack of prints."

"Off topic, but do you want some strawberries? More champagne?"

"I'll have some champagne. Hold on to the strawberries and chocolate for a few more minutes so I can finish this. I'm so close."

Bailey put the empty chicken container back in the basket and pulled out the covered bowl of strawberries. The chocolate sauce was in its own smaller container. He poured more champagne in her glass.

Jasmine sat back on her heels and laid her palette on the grass. She cocked her head. How could someone stare at the same painting so much?

"What are you looking for?"

"I'm looking at the different layers of paint. A bush has to look like a bush, but it also has to fit within the setting. Then, the overall painting must flow. It can't look like different techniques were used."

"Wow. I thought you were about to transport yourself into the lake."

Jasmine giggled then leaned against him. He shifted so she could fit better in the crook of his side. She snuggled in, resting her head on his shoulder. Then he said, "Oh wait."

He opened the lids for the strawberries and chocolate then dipped a large strawberry into the sauce. When he hovered the treat above her, she buried her face in his armpit. He ran the tip of the strawberry along her cheek, making her squirm, and making the chocolate spread from nose to ear. Bailey laughed. Jasmine sat up and wiped her cheek but eliminated only a small portion of the stain.

"Bailey!"

"I'm sorry. Come here; I swear I'll wipe it away." He pulled a roll of paper towels from the basket along with a bottle of water. After pouring water on the corner of a towel, he approached her as if to ask for a truce. Jasmine eyed him with playful suspicion. He slowly wiped the chocolate from her cheek. Bailey kept dabbing at her skin while their eyes locked.

"I think I should be getting back," Jasmine said, the first to break the gaze.

"Yeah. You're so beautiful."

"Thank you."

"Have you ever thought of doing a self-portrait?"

"It's harder to do. I actually have to draw using a mirror."

"You should. You have amazing features: big hazel eyes, a small nose, and an amazing mouth." He leaned forward until he was close enough to kiss her but didn't. She closed the gap. He brought his hand up to cup her sticky cheek.

After a gentle kiss, Jasmine leaned back and said, "We should go."

"You have to let go of me first," Bailey said. Jasmine looked down; her hands were clutching his shirt. She let go and laughed. Bailey gathered the food and put it back in the basket. Jasmine quickly cleaned her brushes, placing them in a plastic bag. She tossed her paints and unused brushes into her messenger bag.

"Ready?"

"Yup."

"Do you need help carrying that stuff?"

"No, I got it."

At Jasmine's apartment, Bailey could tell she wanted to spring up the stairs and shut the door. The tension stifled any words that might make the silence less awkward. Bailey kissed her on the cheek.

"I'll call you tomorrow."

"I have class all day and work tomorrow night."

"Maybe I'll show up at the pub later then."

"Okay, see you then."

"Bye, Jaz."

"Bye, Bailey."

He walked away kicking himself though he wasn't sure why. They'd had an amazing date at the park. It seemed like only a matter of time before annoying habits grated on nerves or fundamental values clashed. As his mind wandered into pessimism, the image of Jasmine laughing returned to him. He remembered the passion in her eyes when she painted, the adorable way she padded around her apartment barefoot and ate peanut butter and jelly sandwiches. Did the future matter if he was already falling in love with her today?

A few days later, Bailey fidgeted in his chair while Jasmine stared at him, clutching a sketch pad in her lap and sitting cross-legged on the floor in her living room. She had been silent for half an hour, and it was definitely making him nervous.

"Hold still."

"You're making me nervous."

"What do you mean? I'm not doing anything."

"Exactly."

"What am I supposed to be doing? I'm trying to draw a picture of you. You agreed to do this. If you want to back out, I can always find another model."

"No, it's okay. I'll try to think of something else."

"Yeah, try that."

Bailey sank deeper into the chair. He arranged his features into his serious face, which only made Jasmine laugh.

"What?"

"Your face has changed. And I know that serious face is not real. Just think about your paper or your family. Wait, don't think about your family."

"I know what you mean."

"Okay. Don't move."

"You are so sexy."

"What? Geesh, Bailey. Why do you keep distracting me?"

"You are adorable with your tongue sticking out like that because you're concentrating so much."

"Shut up!" Bailey slid from his chair and crawled across the floor to her. "What are you doing?"

He pulled the pad from her lap, the pencil from her hand. He set the tools off to the side. Jasmine tried to grab for her stuff and avoid his gaze.

When she tried to scoot backwards, she ran into the wall. Bailey came closer. He kissed her softly until she relaxed. He deepened the kiss, enjoying as her lips widened to welcome him. Jasmine held his face in her hands. Their bodies slid together to the floor. Bailey looked at her for a moment. "You truly are beautiful, Jaz."

"Thank you. Kiss me again."

"Yes, ma'am."

Bailey kissed her deeply. Less time, less care, more need. She reached a hand up his shirt and petted his chest hair. His fingers trailed down her cheek, along her slender neck, over her left breast, felt a trace of her nipple, continued down her stomach, and gripped her thigh to wrap it around his waist. Her other leg wrapped around and her hips began to move against him. He reached up her shirt and slid his hand up her back. The cold surface of the floor on her bare skin was like a bucket of cold water on her face.

"Bailey, stop."

"Jaz…"

"Bailey, seriously."

He stopped, pulled her shirt back down, rolled onto the floor next to her, and stared at the ceiling. He let out a huge sigh and tried to slow his heartbeat.

"Bailey, I'm sorry."

"Don't be. We shouldn't…"

"Not yet."

"Yet?"

"I mean, I want to. You can tell that. But we talked about going slow and making this right. I want that more than I want your naked body."

"Dammit, woman."

She giggled. "Sorry, I couldn't resist." They both lay there, staring at the ceiling, as their breathing slowed.

"Should we get back to the sketch now?"

"If you think you can draw knowing that my blood is still racing because of you."

"I will manage. Sit in the chair, and *don't* get out again."

"Fine."

After adjusting her clothes and sitting back cross-legged, Jasmine picked up her sketchbook. She drew

Bailey for over an hour before he started fidgeting again. To pass the time, he thought of how her body had responded to him at the slightest touch. He soon became restless again, wanting fresh air or a different position.

"Jaz…"

"Okay, okay. You can move. I need a break, too. Do you want something to drink? Eat?"

"No, thanks. Can I see what you've done?"

"No, I don't like to show people my work in progress."

"Yes, but I've seen your work in progress. Show me?"

"Only if you're nice."

"I'm always nice, babe."

"Alright." Jasmine slowly turned the sketchbook. She had captured the shape of his face perfectly: the sharp cheekbones and the subtle curve of his chin. She'd sketched in his nose and eyebrows to allot space for his eyes. Despite the lack of actual features, she had outlined the definitions of his face.

"It's good."

"Don't lie."

"I'm not. I see my facial structure already."

"That's the hardest part for me. I know your eyes so well; they speak to me. I could probably even draw them without you here. Maybe your lips, too. Still, I wouldn't mind your company even if I don't need your face to draw from."

"I will come over. You just have to tell me when."

"Okay. Does this mean you're going?"

"I should. I want to make a few calls, and maybe go to the library to do some research."

"Who do you have to call?"

"My other girlfriends."

"Oh, others? Does that imply that I am one of them?"

"Well, yeah. Anyway, I just want to call my sister to make sure everything is okay. And I need to call Lina; she's been threatening to go back to her ex because she's lonely."

"That's sad."

"You're telling me. He's a jerk. She deserves so much better but can't see it."

"But I bet you try to show her."

"Yes."

"Okay, well I'll call you later."

"Does it bother you that I have a girl for a best friend?"

"No."

"You sure?"

"Yes. It's just unexpected because of you and Jack."

"Well, Lina was there before Jack."

"I know. I respect that you and Lina are close. I hope she is okay."

"She always is; that's the amazing thing about her. She can still get up, brush off her knees, and laugh a little."

"That's awesome."

"Yeah. Alright, babe. I'm going to split. You keep thinking about me and how crazy I drive you late at night."

"Mmmm…will do. Come here." She kissed him quickly. Then she walked him to the door. "Bye, Bailey."

"Later."

"You're so much like your father." Bailey and his mother sat in the den, both reading portions of the weekend's newspaper. At her statement, though, Bailey deflated along with the article he was reading.

"I'm nothing like him. Please don't say that." He tried not to clench his jaw.

"Oh, Bailey. You are smart, strong, an advocate for others, fierce with passion."

"Those are all positive sides to a bad coin, Mom." Bailey looked down at his broad hands and long fingers. His mother leaned toward him and grabbed both within her own. A smile twitched on her lips.

"Bailey, your father has demons. I don't want those same demons to haunt you. You have to be mindful in a way others don't as you go through your life. Don't blind yourself with pride, anger, and self-righteousness." She looked off into the distance, not out the window but to some moment in the past perhaps. "He was so vibrant of character. People were drawn to him. They wanted to hear him speak. He had such opinions about helping people and changing laws to benefit those who struggled."

*"I don't have that same kind of purpose in my life."*

*"You'll get there, love. It takes time."* Bailey looked upon her delicate facial features and saw a hint of the beauty of her younger self. He thought she was done talking. They never openly discussed her marriage or the motivations that make her stay. But she continued, *"I love him, Bailey. I know you don't understand that. But I do. I don't want to be alone. I remember what an attentive man he used to be, and every once in a while, I get a glimpse of that man inside of him. He just doesn't seem to try anymore. I guess…neither do I."*

*Bailey wasn't sure what to say. The power of that kind of love was foreign to him. Maybe love really was blind. It blinds you to the inconvenient truths of when people change for the worse, when a true partnership becomes a codependent cage, and when you've lost yourself to a damaging domestic cycle of violence.*

Bailey decided to walk a different route back to his room. The same streets were starting to bore him, just like the ones in his hometown. He grew restless. His phone rang in his pocket.

"Hello?"

"Hey, stranger."

"What's up?"

"The Boob came to see me last night."

"Lin…"

"I didn't invite him. He just showed up. He apologized for every wrong I put on him."

"Danger. Don't buy it. Men are amazing at sweet talk."

"Trust me. I'm your best friend, aren't I? So, he came over and talked a lot, which is not unusual for him."

"And?"

"I sat there and listened."

"Lina, you're driving me crazy on purpose. Are you delaying telling me that you went back to this guy?"

"I wanted to, Bailey, so much did I want to."

"It's okay. I support you in whatever choice you make."

"But I didn't."

"Yes! I mean, are you okay?"

"I'll be fine. I always manage to get over it, somehow."

"Yes, you do. We all do."

"I think I'm just going to call an escort service and hire a man to have sex with me."

"That's my girl. Now you're talking."

"You *would* encourage me to do something like that."

"Just go out more, Lina. Stop working for one Friday night, unbutton your shirt a little, and go find a man. He will respond if you make yourself available. Men are easy; just show them some cleavage."

"I do have a lot of it."

"Precisely. Go. Do. And don't bite when giving blow jobs."

"No shit."

"Just checking."

"Okay, let me go then. I have to find those men you speak of."

"Alright, babe, good luck. Call me and we can laugh at their sexual inadequacies."

"Deal."

Lina's laughter warmed him. Bailey was about to put away the phone when he saw another call coming in. Man, he was popular tonight.

"Katie?"

"Hey, bro."

"What are you up to?"

"Writing a paper on the American Revolution."

"Do you want to email me the prompt? I can have it to you by morning."

"Want to? Absolutely. Can I? No. Last year, my teacher noticed when you wrote one of my papers; she said I'd contributed in a way I'd never done in class discussion, and that made her suspicious. Plus, I've matured and want to do my own schoolwork. I know; it's shocking."

"Alright. But if you need any help, just call later."

"Sure thing. I'll call you back later tonight."

"Okay. How are things at home?"

"Can't you hear?"

"Actually, no. What's going on?"

"They are going at it. Dad ate the dinner she'd saved for me. I didn't even want the fucking piece of salmon, but he came home and just ate it cold out of the container standing with the door of the refrigerator open. She is flipping out."

"Is he fighting back?"

"What do you think? He is bringing up the fact that she rarely cooks for him anymore, how she no longer does his laundry. Oh! Do you remember that time she found out he'd snuck his underwear in her dirty clothes basket, and she pulled them out of the washer and threw them into the downstairs hallway?"

"Yeah. He made me dry the hardwood floor."

"Yeah, sorry. Oh, here they come. I have to shut my door. Oh shit."

For a moment, Bailey heard loud footsteps and his father whimpering that life hadn't treated him fairly by giving him an inconsiderate wife.

"Are you alright?"

"You know he won't touch me."

"Just checking he hasn't changed his mind."

"Nope. I don't give him the chance. And don't think that the first time he even thinks to raise a hand to my face I won't be on the phone to child services. I'm still a minor."

"Okay. Just be careful, Kat."

"You know I will. But I need to go now."

"Gotcha. I'll give you a factual rundown later."

"Thanks, Bailey. Take care of yourself."

"You, too. Bye."

# CHAPTER FIFTEEN

*Kat*

Kat tossed and turned in bed. Bright red numbers on her clock told her it was only 2:37 in the morning. Ever since Flynn left for Virginia Beach, Kat hadn't slept through the night. She was getting really tired. She could feel herself losing control. She felt empty inside. It was silly that a few weeks with a cute boy had made her think her life could go any way she wanted. Flynn had taught her to enjoy the small moments, the no-hidden-agenda lazy Sundays.

She tried turning to her photography, but she either lost her eye for good composition or just didn't feel inspiration when she was in the darkroom. Even hanging out with Mel only served to remind her of Mel's absent brother.

Kat got out of bed. She padded barefoot downstairs to get a drink. Under the closed door to the den, the blueish tint of the TV caught her eye.

Kat almost turned to go back to her room, but she could tell it was her mother. Her father's distinctive snoring drifted down the hallway. She opened the den door, "Mom?"

"Hi, sweetie. What are you doing awake?"

Kat dropped onto the couch a few cushions from her mother. "I can't sleep."

"Me neither. I can't seem to turn my brain off."

"Yeah, I hear ya." Mother and daughter sat in silence for a moment, until her mother un-paused the recorded show she was watching. Kat recognized actors from the show *Castle*. It was a good show; she had seen this episode on TV earlier in the week.

Kat's mind echoed with all of the questions and secrets left hidden that rested between her and her mother. Would she ever get used to sitting in silence, watching TV, and wasting away the days until she could move out?

"Mom?"

Her mother paused the show again.

"Yes, baby?" Kat moved over a few cushions to sit next to her mother, who put the remote on the side table. "What is it? Something wrong?"

"Nothing specifically. I just don't know what to do."

"About what?" Her mother lifted her arm, and Kat snuggled closer to the warmth of her body. It had been so long since they'd been this close.

"Well, there's this boy."

"A boy? I didn't know. How old is he? Is he in your class?"

"No, he's older. He moved to Virginia Beach a few days ago to be a cop."

"Older? How much older? You better be careful, Katie."

"Mom! Come on. He is only a few years older, and he was a perfect gentleman." Kat suspected the boy talk would not go well, so she tried another tactic. "And I didn't do so well on my SATs."

"You can retake them, right? You'll just have to study harder next time."

"Yeah, I guess. I've taken the test twice already."

"Third time's a charm."

"And Dad's on my case about colleges. I just don't know, Mom. There are too many choices, and I'm so tired. I want to check out."

"Oh, my girl is growing up. I know it's tough. Give yourself a day or two, and then look at it all again. You'll make the right choice."

"How do you know?"

"Because I believe in you. And when you set your mind to it, you can do anything."

"You have to say that because you're my mom."

"Yes, I do. But I also happen to think it's true."

"Thanks, Mom." Kat wasn't sure what she had been hoping to get from the conversation, but it fell short. Maybe she had fallen short. "I'm going to go back to bed; I think I'm tired enough to sleep now."

"Okay. Get some sleep. I'll see you in the morning."

Kat stood up and felt the instant cold from where her mother's body had been. She walked down the hall to her room, knowing she wouldn't sleep. But she had nothing left to say to her mom. After closing her bedroom door, she itched with restlessness. Even writing didn't appeal to her. She wanted to get dressed and go for a walk down the dark neighborhood street, but she'd probably be raped or killed and dumped in the marsh. Flynn was right: She did need to stop reading mysteries.

———⌒———

Kat walked into her house after school and headed for the stairs. She was trying to stay busy now that Flynn had moved, but she desperately wanted some stillness, some silence.

"We need to talk about your future."

She stopped halfway up the stairwell, hand frozen on the wooden banister. Turning her head, she saw her father standing in the doorway of his home office.

"You've been avoiding me."

"Me? No. I've been busy with school and stuff."

"Yes, I know. It's the stuff I'm worried about. I don't approve of your friends and the *stuff* that they do."

"My future? Okay, let's talk."

"I have some interesting brochures I want you to see. They are in my office."

Of course they were. Enter into his domain so he could suck out her soul. Kat hated that office. Dark furniture filled the room, and the rest of the walls and surfaces were crowded with degree diplomas, certificates, and law awards.

In the office, Kat sat in the chair on the opposite side of the desk. She felt like she was in the principal's office, somehow in trouble. Her father plopped a book in front of her: *The Top 400 Colleges and Universities*. "A majority of the schools in that book are in Virginia, so there is no reason for you to go out of state."

With that one statistic, he swiftly eliminated any hope of her attending a school thousands of miles away. He had a tight leash.

"There were actually some schools in New York I was researching. And some in North Carolina."

"Sure, we can discuss those. But I want you to study that book and seriously take a look at the stats for each Virginia school. It's time you get serious about filling out applications and sending them out. You're going to have to make some real decisions about your future."

"I've been thinking about it. I thought maybe teaching or publishing."

"Hmm, yes. A liberal arts school…"

"I thought you said we needed to have a serious talk about this."

"You can't be serious about this. Teachers make shit money, and publishing is a very difficult profession to get into. You have to be dedicated and willing to go way above and beyond normal efforts to get yourself in the door."

"And I am not capable of that level of effort?"

"I didn't say that. I was simply pointing out that it is difficult."

"Fine. I'll read the book. Anything else?"

"Don't get a tone with me, young lady. I will be funding your future education, and I would like a say in the prospects who will set you on your career path."

"Then what would you like me to do with my life, Dad?"

"You can do whatever you want to, Katherine. I am merely pointing out that in all of your fantasies and unrealistic dreams, you consider how you are going to pay your way when I stop supporting you. You need to find a marketable career."

"And sell my soul in the process."

"It's not selling your soul. It's growing up. It's acknowledging that you have to be responsible for your own life."

Kat stifled a chuckle at his last statement. Oh, how the sparks would fly if she pointed out how he should be responsible for his life and the damage caused to those closest to him.

"I expect some appreciation for my gifting you four years of tuition. And I do mean four years. I'm not paying for you to discover yourself in a five-year plan."

"I understand. This has given me a lot to think about. I'm going to go upstairs and read this book. And I'll let you know what I find."

"Yes, perhaps you want to make a spreadsheet of the schools you like, and we can review it when you're done."

"Yeah, I'll be sure to do that."

Kat walked upstairs to her room. Her blood boiled whenever she had to listen to that man. He obviously still felt that he had some sort of authority over her, over this household. In the realm of money, yes, he held tightly to those reins. He made sure that neither Kat nor her mom had any money or any self-esteem to fight back. Kat pulled her cell phone out of her bag to call Flynn.

"Hey, it's Flynn. Leave a message at the beep, and I'll think about calling you back. Maybe."

She knew he was pulling long shifts at work, trying to work hard to impress his boss and his friends. Then when he wasn't on duty, he was sleeping. It made reaching out to him really hard. Kat was being selfish to think that he would be available to her when clearly he was moving on to the next phase of his life. She was proud of him for following his dream. She was glad that he was out helping other people.

Kat could feel the fractured pieces of herself falling away again. Flynn was busy. Bailey was about to have finals. Her parents seemed to be on a completely different wavelength. Even photography was a reminder of failure. She was losing grip on that ledge. If only she could get some sleep.

Kat paced in her room. Her hands crept up into her hair; she was tempted to pull it all out if the relief meant she could sleep. For almost a week she had survived on naps or brief periods of rest, but she wanted to turn off her mind. She wanted to vent to Flynn, but he had sent an email earlier in the day saying he was on a training exercise.

She needed sleep. Serious sleep. Her parents were out at a work function and wouldn't be home until later. It was already midnight. Kat wandered down the hallway, looking from wall to room, hoping to find a solution. She thought of going for a run when she caught a glimpse of her parents' bathroom. There were pills there.

Kat opened random drawers and found the one with the pill-bottle jingle. Tylenol. Motrin. Midol? Oxycodone. Yes. From her mother's visit in the hospital. That would make her relax. She shut the drawer and brought the bottle to her bedroom. She popped the cap off and tipped the bottle to drop a few into her open palm. Maybe she should take more than two? She was really tired. The stark image of the pills made Kat think: How many to turn off her mind forever?

Kat froze as awareness chilled her veins. Her fingertips went numb and began to quiver. She stepped to her nightstand and slowly set the opened bottle down.

She never took her eyes off the half-a-dozen pills in her upturned right hand. Kat picked up the glass of water, illuminated by the dim bedside lamp. She had inherited that lamp—shaped like a flower with a tiny violin-playing angel on a stem leaf—from her grandmother.

Kat's vision began to blur as the little white pills in her palm seemed to merge into one. She raised her hand to her mouth and gulped water to swallow the chalky medicine. The side of her queen mattress depressed as she sat, absorbing the drug into her veins and her mind. The glass rested sideways on her kneecap, her fingers leaving prints in the condensation.

Kat picked up the prescription bottle, which still held plenty of pills. She could take more. She could take them all. Sleeping would solve so many problems: She wouldn't have to look into her father's disappointed eyes, she wouldn't have to be such a burden to Bailey, the family savior, and she wouldn't have to watch her mother live a depressed and unfulfilled life that she was unwilling to change. Her mother's sweet face filled her mind, and tears blurred Kat's vision.

She wouldn't have to feel the ache of Flynn's absence, even though she knew he'd be here with her to coax her to sleep if she asked. She wouldn't have to make all of those seemingly insignificant decisions about her future, when all she truly wanted was to be free.

Kat poured another handful of pills into her palm. There were about ten of them this time. This would definitely silence her mind and its never-ending record of life's expectations. It was just too much pressure; she couldn't breathe. Couldn't they see that she tried every day to be the best version of herself? Couldn't they see she wanted to help her mother find a different life? Couldn't they see she felt so old under the weight of hopelessness and guilt from Hunter's life unlived?

Kat, no matter how hard life seemed, had the distinct advantage of being alive and able to change her life for the better, in honor of her best friend. It was her responsibility to seize Hunter's carefree outlook. What was the point of living if she roamed the streets and halls like an unfeeling zombie, a puppet in the domestic cycle of her parents' manic-aggressive possessiveness? If she got a little sleep, all of the answers would seep through her veins and ease her tense muscles. Maybe then she could release the breath she had stifled for so long.

"Katie! Oh my God! Gregory, come quick!"

Kat was semiconscious of people nearby. She thought she heard her mother's voice, but only as an echo down a long tunnel or muffled like Kat was listening underwater.

She was vaguely aware of strong arms picking her up like a baby or a damsel in distress. Was Flynn here? Did he come back for her? No, he was gone. It wasn't Bailey, either. She felt weightless, drifting through the air.

"It's okay, Katie, baby. We're going to take care of you." A thought surfaced just as her mind drifted to black—it's too late.

# CHAPTER SIXTEEN

## Bailey

*At the funeral, he stood on the outskirts, watching his family mourn in their own ways. He held a single white rose, the bloom hanging down toward the ground. After everyone filed through and departed, he approached her casket. It seemed so small. He looked to the horizon to keep from crying, but out of the corner of his eye, he could still see the dark earth that would bury her in the ground forever.*

*He let the tears fall, and he placed the rose on the lid on top of everyone else's flowers, the white prominent against the pink. He reached out and put his palm against the cool, smooth wood for balance and to touch her one last time. She was too old to tickle, but he should have kept the connection going. He should have been strong enough for the both of them. As memories flushed his brain, he bent his head and cried with all the energy he had left.*

———————◇———————

Bailey awoke from the nightmare with the twitch of a finger. He was sitting in a well-cushioned chair and leaning on the edge of a hospital bed. Kat's hand rested within both of his own. He wouldn't let go of her ever again. His hands still shook from the paralyzing despair from a dream where he'd imagined Kat died, but he sought comfort in her warm fingers. Her eyes fluttered open.

He thought he'd lost her. They barely reached the hospital in time. The doctors pumped her stomach and said she would be in and out of consciousness for a day or so. As soon as Bailey got the call, he'd gone to his professors and asked for an incomplete. Thankfully, he was on relatively good terms with most of them. He could make up the work over the winter break.

"Where am I?" Kat croaked. Her throat was still raw from the intubation tube.

"You're in the hospital."

"Bailey?"

"Yeah."

"Can I have some water?"

Bailey reached for the pitcher of ice water on a rolling end table. He poured some into a plastic cup. His right hand never let go of hers. He held the cup to her mouth, supporting it while she sipped. "What are you doing here?"

"Are you kidding me?"

"You didn't have to come," Kat hung her head and fiddled with the seam of her hospital gown.

"Of course I did. You are my sister. One of the dearest people in my life. When you get so low that you swallow a handful of pain meds, I come, quickly, no questions asked." Bailey rubbed his face with his free hand and looked out the window of the hospital room. He whispered, "Why did you do it?"

"I don't know, Bail. I didn't plan it or anything. I was so tired. And I was sick of all the pain and the lies and the power plays."

"I guess I can understand that. But, jeez, Kat. It's hard enough for me to go day-to-day, but to know that you might die? I couldn't stand that. Promise me you're okay."

"Well, if by okay you mean alive, then yes, I guess I'm okay. But nothing's changed, Bailey. I have to go back into that house now, knowing that Mom thinks I've done the most selfish act and Dad has written me off as a quote 'stupid, fucking, irresponsible, spoiled kid.' He said it was just a ploy for attention."

"Well, we always knew he was an asshole."

"No, it's more than that. I'm done."

"What?"

"I'm done playing their game. I don't care anymore. All along I thought I had to leave their house to be free, but I am just done bending over backwards and sacrificing my own well-being for their approval."

"Kat, come on…"

"No, Bail. It's over. They drove me to this by unloading their spats on me, using me as a middleman in their fights, and then adding to it all the other normal parental criticisms. I am the child. *We* are the children. Tiptoeing around their mood swings and emotionally supporting them through life is a burden I no longer want to take on."

"I wish I could have had such clear vision when I was still living there."

"I'll finish school, and I'll go through the motions. But life will always be this for me unless I change it. I'm finally broken, Bailey." Kat moved her hand from beneath his and reached up to touch his arm. "I want you to know that this is not your fault. There was nothing you could have done. You are still my big brother, and I love you. I feel like I can finally start to rebuild myself... on my own terms."

Bailey stood and hugged her, hard. He felt her strong muscles and bones beneath his grip. His heart mirrored the emptiness within hers.

Someone clearing their throat interrupted their embrace. They both turned to see Flynn standing in the doorway. Kat broke into a tentative smile.

"Hey," Flynn waved. "The nurse said I could come in." He twisted the bill of a navy baseball cap in his hands.

Bailey turned to Kat and explained, "I called him from your phone. I thought maybe you would want him here."

Kat replied, "But he was busy working."

Flynn spoke up for himself, "The training exercise ended, and I got a text that said, 'Come home, I need you.' So when I called you back, Bailey answered and told me you were here."

Bailey straightened out of the chair, finally relinquishing his grip on Kat. "I think I'll go find something stronger than water around here. I won't be far."

"Thank you, Bailey."

"Anytime." He left the room but hovered just outside the door.

Flynn approached the bed.

Kat said, "You could have just called."

"Um, no, I couldn't have. I hear the word 'hospital,' and I'm in my car. Did you forget that I also have a little sister? I would walk through fire to protect her, as I imagine Bailey would as well."

"I thought he was a douche?"

"Yeah, well, maybe not. God, Kat, are you okay?" Flynn sat in the chair and reached for her. She touched his face, and he caught her wrist to kiss her palm. "I was worried. Still am, in fact, seeing you like this."

"I'll be okay. I'm better now that you're here."

"Can I kiss you?" He leaned forward in anticipation.

"No."

"No?"

"I have hospital breath."

"I don't care."

"You really should."

"You want to know why I don't care?"

"Sure."

"Because I love you." With each word, he moved a fraction closer to her before whispering a kiss on her lips. He pulled back to look into her eyes, and his answer glistened in the tears that threatened to fall.

"But..."

"Shh. You need your rest, and I need to talk to your brother." Flynn kissed Kat once more. In the corridor, he found Bailey leaning against the wall opposite Kat's room. "I'm sorry, dude. It's true."

Bailey caught Flynn's direct gaze. "I know."

Flynn nodded.

"But hey," Bailey said, "I need to run to the house to get some things, maybe some of her clothes and stuff. Can you stay here for a while?"

"Absolutely. Go. I'll be here."

"Great. Thanks. I'll just go say goodbye." Bailey returned to the room to catch Kat looking out the window. With Flynn out of sight, he detected the haunted stare that rested beneath the surface of her well-rehearsed façade. Men were strong, their worth determined by how much they could withstand. But a woman's role was to love and bring life and hope into the world. What happens when her spirit is broken?

Bailey kissed Kat on her forehead. She didn't turn toward him. She knew he'd return.

A short while later, Bailey pulled his car into the driveway though he wasn't sure how he managed to get there. He remembered thinking he wouldn't be seeing his house for quite some time, considering the last time he left. He sat motionless in the driver's seat. If he stopped moving, stopped thinking, stopped breathing, maybe then time would stop and he could go backwards. He could go back to a day when Kat was still herself.

Wondering wouldn't reset time or take her pain away. As if with renewed force, a sharp pain seized Bailey's heart, making him gasp. He opened the car door, leaving it open as he walked up the stoop steps and opened the front door. No one was home; there were no sounds, no voices.

Mr. Johnson came around the corner from the kitchen. All of Bailey's pent-up rage, all of his childhood frustrations and fears, balled up into his shaking fists. Bailey's right hand pulled back and then caught his father's left cheekbone.

Bailey snapped back to reality as he saw his father bent over on the floor clutching the side of his face. In disbelief, Mr. Johnson stared up at Bailey. Then rage colored his face. He took his time standing up to face Bailey, still holding his cheek.

"You son of a bitch!"

Taking the insult literally, Bailey pulled his sore hand back and made contact again, this time with one of his father's ribs. He had no idea whether the crack he heard came from the bones in his hand or in his father's torso. He kept hitting—his face, his chest, anywhere, everywhere.

It didn't matter anymore. In his mind, he was already gone, already back in his car driving to a place where he could be alone.

Bailey didn't glance back at his father's crumpled body in the living room. Out of the corner of his eye, he saw his mother crouched on the steps, staring with wide eyes. He turned to look at her. He should have softened his gaze, loosened his fists, maybe taken a steady breath, but he didn't. His last image of his mother would be terrifying: It would haunt him to see her eyes tear up as she recognized who he was.

<hr />

Lina found Bailey's dorm room door unlocked. She let herself in, surprised that all of the lights were off except a lamp in the back. She crept toward the light, calling out to her friend, "Bailey?"

She continued toward the light and stepped into Bailey's bedroom. The lamp on his desk illuminated a photograph of his mother and sister. Lina's throat constricted. She was about to turn around when she glimpsed his plaid comforter leaning against the dresser, a head peeking out from underneath and a bare foot resting nearby on the floor.

"Oh, Bail…"

He looked up. He had no more tears or anger. All that remained was a haunted stare. He only heard her voice.

"Lina."

She walked around the edge of the blanket and sat beside him. She lightly touched the corner of the plaid blanket and snuggled underneath next to him. Bailey continued to stare across the room at the illuminated photograph.

His mind was too far away, even as his body warmth seeped through her clothes.

She brushed his overgrown hair out of his face. He blinked at her touch but made no other movement. Without words, she rested her head on his shoulder and adjusted her body to fit snug with his.

Eventually, her own vision began to lose focus. She came to accept the still, gray cloud that became his bedroom as if they existed in nothingness. She sighed, and ever so slowly his hand, wrapped in an ACE bandage, emerged to grasp hers.

# EPILOGUE

*Four Years Later*

K at knocked on the door of the new house. Jasmine answered, smiling a greeting.

"Kat, please come in!" Bailey walked up behind Jasmine to say hello. As Kat crossed the threshold, Bailey enveloped her in a full-body embrace. There was no awkwardness now. They had both healed themselves and had come to find peace.

"Welcome to my new home."

Jasmine closed the door and turned toward them. "Our new home."

"Yes, yes, how could I forget?"

They walked through the foyer and made their way into a large two-story living room. "Wow, this is nice."

"You are welcome any time."

"Are you kidding? I'm a junior now, Bail. You remember, I'm going to be spending all my time in the library." Bailey and Jasmine shared a private smile.

"But, Kat, you're a business management major."

"Yes, and my final project is to create a business model that can survive in any city or town."

"And?"

"Well, so far I've got a sketch for a women's shelter."

Jasmine replied, "That's a fabulous idea. It would support any kind of community."

"Let me know if you need any help with it. I am a teacher, after all." Bailey puffed out his chest with pride.

"Yeah, of history." They laughed.

"Dinner is almost ready. Let's go check out the kitchen."

As they walked around a granite bar island, Kat smelled the lasagna in the oven. Jasmine asked, "Will Flynn be joining us?"

"No. Unfortunately, his transfer papers are still being processed. He's hoping that everything goes through by winter break so we can look for an apartment in downtown Charleston."

"Oh, that would be nice." Jasmine grabbed the potholders on the counter and bent to open the oven door. She pulled out a family-sized dish of lasagna.

"I'm getting excited for him to be down here with me." Kat smiled, and Bailey's heart lightened. "But I know I have to focus on finals first."

"Oh, babe. Is your old apartment still up for rent?" Bailey pulled plates from the cabinets and carried a loaf of garlic bread wrapped in tinfoil to the kitchen table.

"I think so? I'll ask around. I loved that apartment. Great light for painting."

As the night progressed, the dinner conversation turned to schedules and tales of the classroom. Kat felt the faint echo of a similar dinner with the stories of a passionate teacher, and she knew her brother would be an inspiration to his students. Soon, they would all be making their homes here in South Carolina, by the water, in a town of history and hope for the future.

CPSIA information can be obtained
at www.ICGtesting.com
Printed in the USA
BVHW091052010521
606210BV00019B/2169/J

9 781736 298213